DEDICATION

Fatty 50
Julie 60
Dad 80

Happy Birthday

CONTENTS

PART ONE

CHAPTER ONE 1

CHAPTER TWO 14

CHAPTER THREE 24

CHAPTER FOUR...33

CHAPTER FIVE 40

CHAPTER SIX 50

CHAPTER SEVEN 62

CHAPTER EIGHT...69

CHAPTER NINE 76

PART TWO

CHAPTER TEN 89

CHAPTER ELEVEN 95

CHAPTER TWELVE 103

CHAPTER THIRTEEN 113

CHAPTER FOURTEEN 124

CHAPTER FIFTEEN...132

CHAPTER SIXTEEN 144

CHAPTER SEVENTEEN...156

CHAPTER EIGHTEEN 160

PART THREE

CHAPTER NINETEEN 162

CHAPTER TWENTY 164

CHAPTER TWENTY-ONE...168

CHAPTER TWENTY-TWO 178

CHAPTER TWENTY-THREE 180

CHAPTER TWENTY-FOUR.....................................181

PART ONE

CHAPTER ONE

'That is your gift,' she said.

'What?' I asked.

'Being able to sit and do nothing.' She replied enigmatically.

'I'm good at doing nothing or not good at doing anything?' I knew she didn't mean that. We'd been married long enough.

'Don't twist my words.' She was telling me off now.

'OK,' I said and gave up.

She kissed me on the cheek, I turned to try and steal one on the lips but she was already gone into the kitchen. When she returned with a plate of meat paste sandwiches with the crusts cut off and a pot of tea, I had to wonder if it was maybe my birthday.

'Is there a special occasion dear?' I asked.

'No, I'm just happy darling. Shouldn't we open these windows and maybe put the cricket on? I'll take the dog for a walk and then you won't have to worry.'

I started to think that early retirement might not have been such a bad plan after all and toyed with the idea of grabbing a book to read while the cricket was on, or perhaps I could just think about putting pen to paper on my memoirs? I reached for another sandwich.

It was a beautiful day for a walk with a breeze coming across the hills from the west, straight from the sea. Arthur, a Cocker Spaniel, would love it and want to run off and chase rabbits and pheasants, real or imaginary. We couldn't quite see the coast from our bungalow's French windows but the horizon hinted at it beyond the facing neighbours' farm. I didn't want to question why Peggy was so energetic today she had always been like that from time to time ever since we met. This Peggy was much preferable to the one who had moods, when I suspected she would think about our son who had died young. Just then the phone rang, and I picked it up thinking it might be Peggy again.

'Hello darling,' I said.

'It's not darling I'm afraid,' a rather cynical voice put paid to my frivolity. 'And I think you know who this is and why I'm calling. How is retirement suiting you?'

A chill ran down my spine and my heart started to race. I slammed the phone down, flushing. Was it possible, after all these years? I wished now that I could have taken Arthur for a turn down the hill into the village, and had a pint or two. I could run after Peggy maybe? But then she'd know something was wrong. I wrote a note about quickly dashing to the shops and left it in the porch where we kept spare keys in a cut-glass bowl.

The pub, and any ensuing row with Peggy, would be small potatoes compared to the plan I now had to put in place and quickly: The plan to save our lives. If I was being watched, they would also know where Peggy was. We would have to disappear in plain sight. Leaving the house and going for a drink to clear my head would be a very predictable reaction to the phone call and wouldn't look out of place to the watchers. I closed and locked the French windows, locked the front door and went down the hill towards the village.

As soon as Peggy let Arthur off the lead he tore into the nearest ditch and scrambled up the far bank through the nettles and the hedge to emerge out of her reach in a newly ploughed field. She started to call him but knew it was in vain so early in the walk. He could be gone for hours. He was already miles away entering a copse at the top of the field. Pheasants rattled as they were flushed from cover. Her heart sank.

Also watching Arthur's progress was a slightly anxious man in camouflage who had no doubt that a Cocker Spaniel could smell him a hundred yards away. 'Fuck off dog,' he said out loud. Harold had served in Iraq and Afghanistan so the dog didn't pose a threat exactly but he would have to kill it if it was going to give away his hiding place, and besides he liked dogs. He would more likely kill its owner but Harold didn't see the paradox.

My escape and evasion plan had been in place for years but had never been put to the test. I walked into the pub and ducked to avoid hitting my head on the horse brasses that hung over the medieval lintel.

'Hello John,' the landlord greeted me. A nice lad who'd moved here with his young wife and daughter. You could tell that the wife was bored and restless, always making eyes at men who came into the pub. She was attractive in a very village-pub way and he, the husband, seemed oblivious to all the attention she got. I couldn't see her, though. 'Usual?' he said disinterestedly.

'Please, thanks. Have you got any of those pasties?' They came from Cornwall and sometimes got a bulk load in if they'd done a family trip home.

'I think there's a few left in the back. You want one for lunch? Should I warm it up?' With one hand still on the pump and the other holding my pint glass he looked over his shoulder to an invisible helper in the kitchen.

'No thanks I've got a few friends coming and wanted to help Peggy with the food. I need five or six I think, please.'

I downed my pint of bitter, ordered another, and glanced around. No watchers in the boozer but it was impossible to see much of the street through the low-slung bay windows and bubbled glass.

'Cheers,' I paid for the pints and pasties in cash trying to remember if I was going to need coins or notes later. Maybe I should have swiped. As I closed the door of the pub behind me I thought I saw a flash of light, like light on a glass lens, from the edge of the trees in the field above. It was enough to confirm my suspicions.

In the village shop I bought toilet roll, juice, bottled water, crisps, cheese, chocolate, apples and bread. And a newspaper. To them it would have looked like a normal weekend top-up. As an afterthought I threw in a lucky dip for Wednesday's Lottery and a can of beans. The beans tipped me over the balance of normal and Beryl the shopkeeper raised an eyebrow.

'We're expecting guests and neither of us really wants to cook.' I said as nonchalantly as possible.

'I know the feeling, John dear. How's Peggy?' Beryl managed.

'Fine, thank you. She's just gone into the fields to walk Arthur.'

'Yes I thought I saw him in the distance a few minutes ago.' Ever the busy-body, there was nothing Beryl didn't know.

'Oh really? Where was that?' me, feigning disinterest.

'That copse. The one behind Robin Hood's Hut,' she slid the till shut with both hands.

That one where the sun caught the movement of a camera lens I thought. 'Well, it's a beautiful day maybe I'll go and join them. Thanks Beryl, give our love to Bill.'

There's a path back to the cottage through the churchyard and along a different lane that runs next to an old mill stream. I took it and hoped I would bump into Peggy and Arthur on their way back to the house and I quickened my pace. I reached the back door only to be disappointed that Arthur wasn't there to greet me panting with wet fur and bramble twigs knotted into his belly hair. I imagined Peggy running up behind him calling his name, worried that he might get run over by a car because she hadn't been able to get the lead back on. No sign of Peggy either. I left my shoes by the back door out of habit and went inside straight to the front porch where I found my note unread. I crumpled it up and chewed it before swallowing. Next I cleaned my teeth, first turning the cricket back on and opening the French windows. It was the Channel 5 coverage which I liked. The shopping went into a sort of duffel-type travel bag I had for weekends away if I travelled with work, along with a few things I thought Peggy would need and a bottle of wine and a half bottle of whiskey. I also slipped in a package that I had hoped we might never need. We were going to need a drink before the end of this night. I carefully went back outside to the back door of the garage – no sign of movement in the treeline above the field – and put the bag on the back seat of the car. I didn't want to have to stop and open the boot if we needed the contents while we were driving. Chances were that we wouldn't be stopping much. The asbestos-built garage had caught the heat of the afternoon and smelled of lawn mowers and oil. Perhaps I'd be gardening later if I hadn't had that phone call. Then it occurred to me that maybe I should do a spot of gardening and I dug out my gloves and pruning shears. I also put out our little table and chairs with a bird book and a pair of binoculars.

Having lost the toss England then lost two wickets in the first two balls. It was going to be a long weekend.

'Arthur. Arthur, for the love of God. There's biscuits at home Arthur. Come on, boy!'

Peggy had not wanted to go as far as the copse. It was nearly tea time and the climbing was not good for her knees and hip. She wanted to be at home with John thinking about what to cook for dinner. She went as far as Robin Hood which was already much farther than she'd wanted and now she felt tired and frustrated. Of course to Arthur it was all a big game but even he was too old for such larks and would pay the price later, probably sleeping on his doggie beanbag the whole day tomorrow.

'OK, I'm going to leave you, silly boy. Come home when you're ready. You know the way.' She broke out of the tree line in front of the Landmark Trust owned ex-hunting lodge which was just catching the start of sunset and took the most direct path back along the fields to their back door.

Harold, or 'Harry', liked Arthur and used all of his strength to keep him quiet and still as the dog kicked and desperately wanted to respond to his mother's call. He let Peggy get about a hundred yards further away and then released the Spaniel who immediately turned on him and started to bark and growl. Harry had thought that he would just bounce off down the fields in search of biscuits; his weakness for dogs was now going to come back and bite him in the arse.

I thought I heard Arthur barking and growling, which was unusual so my ears were instantly alerted. I stopped pruning and picked up the binoculars training them to where I'd seen the lens flash earlier. Coming towards the house I saw Peggy and my heart leapt with relief. She had also heard Arthur and stopped in her tracks to turn and look. The afternoon light was now catching the façade of Robin Hood's Hut. Peggy started back up towards the trees. In certain situations you have to trust your instincts and training. What I did next was done in the blink of an eye but it felt like a year and a half as if I was swimming in glue or running in slow motion. Table and chairs away. Binoculars with me. TV on low. Curtains drawn or open? Half-drawn. Internal lights on in bedroom and bathroom and kitchen, just in case. Doors and windows locked. One last trip to the garage, into the car and up the hill to the woods. Driving might take five or ten minutes normally but right now I didn't have that luxury. I drove recklessly knowing that there would be little or no traffic at this time of day on a Saturday.

Peggy could clearly see Arthur now but she'd never seen him so aggressive and wondered if he'd maybe found a fox or a badger.

'Come on Arthur, leave whatever it is you've found alone please.' She used her assertive no-nonsense voice. He cocked his head and thought about coming. But didn't.

With the car in four-wheel-drive, high range I sped up the hill and smashed through the wooden gate into the ploughed field. The hidden gunman fired two shots at the windscreen, which probably saved Peggy's life for which I was grateful. Peggy couldn't quite believe what she was seeing and didn't know how to react. She froze. The dog, recognising the car and scared by the shots started to run towards me. I sped across the ploughed surface and stopped next to my wife, opened the door and signalled for her to get in and get down. The dog sprang straight up and into the back before I'd even opened the boot. I could see the shooter standing up in the copse now, his camouflaged silhouette familiar from a past life. I opened my door, rolled to the right and squeezed off two shots in quick succession from a kneeling position before rolling again and sprinting in a crouch position towards his cover. As I reached the trees I could see his outline retreating along the hedgerow towards the next gate. 'I must have hit him,' I thought, 'why is he running?' I caught my breath and steadied my aim with both hands, planted my feet shoulder-width apart and was just about to take him out when I saw the garish fluorescent pink tabards of a cycling club cresting the hill from the other direction. It wouldn't do for either of us to be caught up in a fracas involving the public and so I also ran, for my car.

'Are you OK? Are you hit?' I asked Peggy, who I could see was still in shock. 'Are you OK boy?' I glanced back at Arthur but he was excited and panting. At the gate I gambled that the cyclists hadn't seen or heard anything untoward and waited for them to pass securing it as best I could behind me. For all they knew we might very well be the land owners in our muddy little Disco with a wet spaniel in the back.

9

I owed Peggy an explanation but that would have to wait until I'd contained the current situation. 'We're not going to go straight home, love. We can't go home.' I drove down the hill and drove past, through the village towards the main A road which in turn would take us to the motorway. If I was right about the man being injured he would have to get help and not follow us in broad daylight which would be inherently dangerous, and if I was him I'd much rather regroup and come back with more men and a better plan. Actually, thinking about it I realised that Arthur must have unearthed him during the surveillance phase of their op. In that respect it was our lucky day.

'Good dog, good boy! Clever boy!' I said out loud to the rear-view mirror.

I changed Radio 3 to Radio 5 Live Sports Extra to check the cricket and I glanced at Peggy, squeezing her right hand with my left as I drove. Six for six!! Disaster; I flicked to CD with my right index finger from the controls on the steering wheel. Peggy still said nothing and after thirty minutes she fell asleep. An hour and a half later as glimpses of the sea appeared over the horizon we were nearly there. England had rallied a little bit by taking a few early wickets after lunch. Safely off the motorway I let Arthur out to have a pee, filled up with fuel and bought some more snacks. Stopping was a calculated risk; I paid cash and waited long enough to make sure that we hadn't been followed, even at a distance. Confident that we were alone, I took the B road to the seaside resort, through town with its promenade and kiss-me-quick pier and parked off the main street in a secluded cobbled courtyard. I unpadlocked the sliding wooden doors, turned off the alarm and revealed our safe house.

'Drink?' I said to Peggy, kissing her lightly on the forehead. Arthur wagged his tail and sniffed the new surroundings. I pulled two tumblers down from a cupboard above the sink and poured us a both a whisky from the bottle in the duffel bag.

As I sipped mine, Peggy downed hers and indicated that she wanted another one.

'It's very yellow,' she said drily. And then, 'Arthur needs a proper walk.'

Looking round the rather twee kitchen I had to agree, especially now as the sun cast its golden hour rays through the lace-curtained window. I flicked on the digital radio and noticed that a nightwatchman had come in; it was a good sign meaning that we must have got a few wickets.

Grabbing Arthur's lead from where I'd hung it by the door, Peggy turned to ask, 'I suppose it's safe to go out?' There was the merest hint of a grin beneath the angry veneer and sarcasm.

'Yes, come on,' I said, 'let's go. Fish and chips OK?'

I left Peggy and Arthur running up and down the wide expanse of beach and mud flats where I could see them from the window of the chip shop on the other side of the road. I paid cash and we all sat down to eat, including Arthur. 'God he's going to get diarrhoea,' I thought. And we watched the sun set over the sea.

When we got home Arthur fell fast asleep in his new dog basket and started snoring. I laid a small fire in the log burner to heat the hot water and when I stood back up Peggy was framed in the doorway completely naked. 'I didn't know you had a gun, Johnny!' she said, tugging at my belt.

We made love in the open plan living-room-cum-kitchenette and then lay down as best we could in the little bedroom. It was cosy and we cuddled up in a way that took us both back at least thirty years.

'So what are you, Johnny? Some sort of spy?' she asked.

'I'll tell you as much as I can love, but that's not a lot. The less you know the better.'

'I want to know everything, Johnny. You were always a little bit quiet, but I never imagined all *this* under the surface.'

'It's dangerous Peggy, that's why I never told you. Except now they're coming after me.'

'Don't you think I have a right to know?'

'It's not that simple. They could have killed you today, you and Arthur, for stumbling on them like that. If they think you know anything they'll want to get it out of you.'

'Who are *they* Johnny?' She was raising her voice now. 'Who are *you*?'

'I'm the good guys.'

'What have you done? Why do they want to kill you? Why would *anybody* want to kill *you*?'

'Why indeed?' I muttered to myself.

Then we both fell asleep.

CHAPTER TWO

The next morning I woke up early and tiptoed out of the house without waking the wife or the dog. I wanted to go for a run but also needed to check a few things before putting phase two into action. I strapped the pistol, a Browning Hi-Power I'd had since the beginning under my thermal running top using the shoulder holster and left the house, bolting the sliding doors behind me. The gun was loaded again and the safety on – I'd checked. The beach was deserted and I did a quick loop up into the dunes and back before making my way to the marina. I hadn't run on sand for a while and it was tough on my calves. I couldn't see anybody or any vehicles that looked out of place, and was in fact pretty confident they wouldn't find us here unless we stayed too long.

The private harbour where I kept my boat was more managed moorings than yacht club and I hoped I'd be early enough not to bump into anybody. I made my way down to the boardwalk wharf and didn't see anybody in the harbour master's cabin as I passed it. The sea and the sky were calm, with only the occasional breeze slapping cables against masts as I neared my mooring. A shape, unmistakably a man emerged from what could easily have been my boat, *Oystercatcher*, judging by the location. My heart skipped a beat. As he recognised me and gave a guilty smile I realised I was not imagining it and my mind raced through a million possibilities in a split second. I half raised my arm towards my gun but wanted to give him – the harbour master – the benefit of the doubt. Although, having said that he knew me as a policeman which was a small white lie and I could have been forgiven for carrying a weapon. I instinctively looked behind me and saw to my horror another man stepping onto the gangway, carrying something that looked very like a gaff hook.

My morning run had warmed me up and I reacted fastest of the three, unholstering my weapon and shooting the harbour master in the shoulder before anybody had time to ask questions. He fell to the ground, wounded not dead. The second man was now close enough to try and smash me with the long-handled fish hook, but I blocked his blow with my right forearm and the pistol fell to the planks. He lunged and tried to impale me but I grabbed it, moved to one side and used the momentum to pull him close enough to kick him into the sea. Peggy and Arthur were in imminent danger and I ran as fast as I could back home, not caring that I'd left both of my assailants alive: I knew that these were hired muscle or informants and couldn't see them posing any further threat.

From the marina it was a short uphill sprint back to the seafront and the little hidden courtyard beneath the old sailmakers' loft. I went through the archway, turned the corner and found both padlocks smashed, the sliding door left open and the house of course was empty. My heart sank, I couldn't breathe and had to catch my breath before banging my fist on the yellow draining board and shouting, 'Shit, shit, shit!' Next to the digital radio my mobile phone began to vibrate and ring. Caller ID said it was Peggy. After a deep breath I took the call, a voice not Peggy's answered:

'Now you know we are not playing games,' it was a man's voice and I instinctively strained my ears for any background noises, 'if you want to see your family again

15

you must bring what we want. You have twenty-four hours.'

'That's impossible,' I said trying to sound as composed as possible, 'I don't have it.'

'Then you'd better get it.'

'I'll need an extra day and if you harm a hair on any of their heads, including the dog, the deal's off. Understood?'

'Understood.'

'At which point I'll come for revenge.'

'I don't think you're in a position to make threats.'

'I want proof they're alive, let me speak to Peggy.'

There was a pause with indistinct rustling. I tried to find something, anything familiar in the noises, then suddenly my wife, 'John, please come and help us for God's sake John, please!!'

'I will love, I will I promise.'

The phone was wrestled away from Peggy and the man's voice came back on, 'You have forty-eight hours. We'll be in touch.' Now I really did want the dog to get the shits.

I couldn't believe they had Peggy now. For a split second I thought of our daughter Karen when he said family but she was happily married in Australia and safely away from this mess I hoped. And why take the dog, to try and piss me off? They'd called me using Peggy's mobile

16

but I dialled our landline on impulse to see if that's where they'd gone and maybe somebody would pick up. No answer. It didn't look good. How had they found her? How had they found me? I'd successfully lived under this and other aliases for fifteen years and was trained in counter espionage and evasion techniques – I wasn't easy to find. Had I underestimated my enemy or had they just got lucky? Thank God I'd left the harbour master and his crony alive; I now desperately needed to talk to them both. I didn't have what the kidnappers wanted and had no intention of risking my life to get it, or at least I wouldn't risk my life to get it and give it to *them*. My only chance of getting out of this alive and saving my family was to find them first and launch a surprise attack, but in order to do that I needed information.

Before jumping in the Land Rover I checked as well as I could for booby traps. Nothing I could see underneath or under the bonnet. Why had they left me the car, because they were in a hurry? Yes, I concluded, yes. Neither Peggy nor Arthur would have gone without a fight and I'm sure it was the last thing on their minds. Plus if they urgently needed me to get what they wanted, I'd need transportation. I drove sedately through town and then put my foot down on the sand-blown track leading back to the marina. There was a stiff breeze but it wasn't raining. It was Sunday morning and there were very few people around. Too early for sightseers and the few fishermen still operating locally had either already set out or weren't back yet.

This time I drove straight down the slipway and parked outside the office. After a quick glance around I burst through the door gun-in-hand to find the harbour master bandaged but still bleeding reclining at his desk trying to breathe.

'Who contacted you and how? I need answers.' I said. 'Your paymasters have kidnapped my wife and dog. Why were you on my boat this morning?' I stopped short of wringing his neck, but there was no need. I could already see the life draining out of his face.

'I've called an ambulance.' He managed. I could hear the wail of the siren but it still sounded far away.

'And your friend?' I enquired looking round the small quarters and checking through the curtains that he wasn't nearby outside.

'Gone,' it sounded like an honest answer. 'No. I mean he died. He couldn't swim.' Now I knew he was lying and the friend would be back. I went behind the desk and threatened him with another shot.

'No please, please don't. I didn't want any trouble. They said it was easy money. Just telling them when you came and went. Nothing else, I swear.' He was sweating now, feverish cold sweats.

'Did they pay you well?' I was genuinely interested for a second, 'How much?' I shouted in his ear and applied pressure to the wound as the ambulance got closer to the town. He writhed in agony and tears welled in his eyes. 'Who set it up? I need a name or a number, anything. Or you die right here, simple as that.'

'James. He runs a gallery. That's all I know. Please.' He managed, gasping for air. I eased off the pressure and left keeping an eye on him and the door behind me as I backed out. No sign of the friend yet and I was anxious to make myself scarce. As I pulled out of the bay once more I thought to myself, 'Yes, I know James. He's my landlord but how the hell would he know that I have any kind of double existence?' The questions were piling up faster than the answers.

With the safe house now compromised I wondered if going back home was paradoxically safe now? I needed more weapons and technical equipment which were hidden at home plus clothes other than the ones I'd packed for going on the lam by boat. It would also let me know once and for all whether or not Peggy and Arthur were being held there or not. Hiding in plain sight was a tried and tested method going back millennia. But first I wanted to track down James and then I wanted to sneak a look at the yacht; I might as well stay here for the time being. From the security camera covering the courtyard, before they disabled it, and concealed surveillance cameras on the car I had a good idea of who'd snatched Peggy and Arthur and a partial number plate to go on. It might be enough to track their movements after I'd confronted James. If I had to guess I'd say the driver was the man I shot in the copse but that would mean either he'd had no treatment for his wound or that in fact I hadn't hit him. I felt they were nearby, that was my hunch, but in theory they could have been absolutely anywhere. But as any computer programmer will tell you we humans are not unpredictable. The harder we try to create randomness the more obvious and predictable we become, which was what I was banking on.

Looking at the smashed up padlocks I discarded them and fixed the broken alarm with tools I had in the Land Rover. After rewiring the security camera and locking myself in the house I made a cup of tea and spread out a map of the county on the yellow table. I showered and shaved quickly and changed into some comfortable cords, checked shirt and light jacket. There wouldn't be any cricket coverage until closer to lunchtime so I put on Radio 3 instead. Dunking digestives into my tea I started to feel a bit more human and ready to face James and start tracking Peggy. The map made me feel confident that whatever head start they had didn't matter that much as they were only going to hole up somewhere nearby and wait for me to deliver. I still needed to know what the harbour master had done to my boat, if anything, and then I'd be free to vanish.

It was unlikely that James would be in his gallery on a Sunday, and certainly not this early but I knew he sometimes lived in the flat upstairs, even at the weekend, so it was definitely worth ringing the bell. I was slightly concerned that the injured henchman could have tipped him off but that was a chance I was willing to take. With the Browning tucked into its holster under my arm I turned off the engine and scanned the street outside James'. It was deserted, narrow, cobbled, and pretty. There would be tourists later if the weather held. No lights on downstairs but the upstairs curtains were open which made me think he might be in although I couldn't see his car parked outside. I put on a tweed cap and made my way to the glass side-door which led upstairs to the private residence. The rattan blind was pulled three quarters of the way down and I could see uncollected post on the doormat. I rang the doorbell but there was no answer. It looked like a single Yale lock which I might be able to jimmy with a credit card. Checking over my shoulder and looking round again I felt confident no one could see me and forced the door open. I just had time to hear the sound of running water when the alarm went off. I froze. There must be different zones for up and down, I thought. Not seeing the control box nearby I sprinted upstairs as quietly as possible and found the panel on the landing, silencing the alarm. With my heart pounding in my chest I sat in the armchair waiting with my gun aimed at whoever might emerge from the shower.

The water stopped and then the bathroom door opened. A young blonde woman stepped out with a towel held across her body, drying her face and hair. Without seeing me she turned away and I watched her buttocks disappearing into the kitchen. Singing she switched on the kettle and the radio, and I heard cupboard doors opening. As quietly as I could I went back downstairs and let myself out. I waited two minutes to get my breath back and then rang the bell again.

'Who is it please?' her voice enquired through the intercom.

'I'm looking for James is he in? I'm a friend and a tenant actually.' Had I been wearing one I would have straightened my tie.

'Hang on, I'll buzz you in.'

The door clicked open and I stood in the stairwell for the second time.

'Hi,' she said, 'come up.'

'Hi,' I replied, and ascended.

The girl was very pretty with high cheek bones and a mischievous mouth, dressed in shorts and a tee-shirt with no bra I couldn't help noticing, she continued to dry the ends of her long blonde hair with the towel I'd seen earlier.

'I'm Jane,' she smiled, extending her hand. 'James' daughter, excuse the mess.' Her arm swept the room taking in an unmade futon, overflowing ashtrays and newspapers in its arc.

'John, pleased to meet you.' I replied. 'Just tell him I called if he's not around, no problem.'

Jane lit a cigarette and inhaled smiling at me. She exhaled and said, 'Coffee? I've just made a pot and Sundays at the flat are *so* boring. Sit down if you can find somewhere.' She was in the kitchen now. 'Daddy's disappeared, actually. And I'm pissed off with him as a matter of fact.' She emerged with two mugs of coffee and no towel, the cigarette between her lips. 'God,' she sighed. 'Well at least you're here. Like an angel sent to entertain me or something.'

'When you say disappeared?' I ignored the other comment.

'He stood me up the bugger. We were supposed to have dinner together last night and he was *supposed* to give me my allowance, but nothing nada, rien. I waited for two bloody hours in that stupid fucking restaurant.'

'Which restaurant is that?'

'The Lobster Pot, or whatever it's called.' She stared blankly out of the window and took another drag.

'Ah, I see,' my mind racing. 'And you tried phoning?'

'Of course, but he's still not bloody answering. Bastard.'

'You don't think something might have happened to him?'

'To Daddy? *God* no.' Jane threw her head back and laughed, stubbing the cigarette out in one of the many ashtrays.

'And when did you last see your father, Jane?'

'He was here on Friday, in the shop I mean.'

I stood up, ready to move on. 'Thanks for the coffee and nice to meet you.'

'Stay if you like?' She said almost absently, raising her eyes to meet mine. She had green eyes and they reminded me of the sea for some reason.

I half-wavered then said, 'I'm sure Daddy will turn up tomorrow morning.' And I ran down the stairs. As I got into the Land Rover and started the engine I could see her watching me from the window. I waved goodbye and said under my breath, 'turn up dead, probably.'

CHAPTER THREE

I decided then and there not to waste another day and night waiting for darkness to go and see the yacht. Instead I'd risk going now but would have to be in disguise, or at least make myself as invisible as possible. I wished I'd had the dog with me to walk along the strand and use that as cover but I also had some things in my duffel which would help. I drove back to the yellow mews and got ready. I thought about Peggy, and Jane, and the dog. I hadn't seen James on the CCTV but that didn't mean he wasn't involved with the kidnapping. But I'd known him for several years and found it hard to see him as anything more than someone they'd tried to use to get to me. Of course I could be wrong but for me he was already dead. Dead, along with the harbour master.

With long hair and a beard I barely recognised myself in the mirror. A thick-knit woolly hat and black donkey jacket, which had hung on the peg in my bolt-hole since I'd first rented it, completed my subterfuge. My own wellington boots and a slight stooped shuffle completed the look. I drove as close as I dared to the marina and making sure no one was about hid the Land Rover from view behind a dune before approaching. No ambulance but there was a marked police car parked at an angle in front of the office, which was now roped off with incident tape. 'Fair enough,' I thought.

I took stock of my situation and tried as quickly as possible to formulate a plan of action. One of the first boats inside the fence was an old wooden dinghy with oars roped to a ring in the stonework before the wooden jetty left the mainland. I decided to head straight for it and row towards my boat. I had to assume that my disguise was convincing and went for it, clambering down into the wooden craft as only an old sailor could. No shouting police behind me just the gentle lap of the waves and the shrill call of the gulls. Sunday morning and still few people around although casting my eyes through the boardwalk uprights to the main beach I could see more joggers, windsurfers and dog walkers out and about. As I cast off and prepared to row I heard an outboard start up simultaneously with its bup-bup-bup metronome kept at low revs. From my low vantage I couldn't see which berth it came from yet, but my senses were on high alert.

After a couple of minutes *Oystercatcher*, my thirty-eight-footer, hove into view. She might have been my pride and joy in other circumstances but was merely functional now, waiting to take me away to safety when the time came. That time was now and I was forced to think back on how we had reached this point, which events had set in motion this chain of crime and pain that we were now experiencing. Yet there was no time to dwell and all I could do was rely on my instincts to persevere and overcome. Then I saw it, a white angled keel at roughly my eye line. I stood up and dove aboard my boat's bow-ladder to get a better view as the launch headed out to open water. Had it tried to ram me in the dinghy? I wasn't sure but still alive and unharmed had to think not. A warning maybe? Why warn me when you've already captured my wife? Just my imagination, then. I went to look around the boat.

No sign of a break-in, the hatch was still locked and I opened it pushed it back and pulled open the little saloon doors to enter down the steep companionway steps. If the harbour master had riffled through my possessions on James' orders, looking for something I didn't possess he'd either done a very bad job or done a very good job of putting everything back in its place. I think the latter with hindsight, the *Oystercatcher* looked neater and cleaner than I remembered. A couple of reasonably expensive oils that I'd collected over the years, I was pleased to see them again, and a few family photos. The cabins and galley were also shipshape. Up in the cockpit I was less certain that he hadn't had his grubby hands all over it looking for something. The laptop was open, cupboard doors left ajar and the chart drawer wide open. The radio was on and I instinctively switched it off to conserve its charge. This must have been when he'd clocked me pulling up in the Land Rover, no doubt alerted by the missing sidekick. I took the ignition key out of my pocket and turned her over, the twin Volvo inboard diesels both sounding in good voice, which was good news but I'd paid the harbour master a little extra to keep her sea-ready. That is before I shot him.

Taped to the back of the bottom left-hand drawer were a key and a memory stick which I now rescued and put safely in my inner pocket. I'd forgotten that I was dressed as an old sea-dog until the thick coat reminded me. Satisfied I locked up *Oystercatcher* and made my way back to the dinghy. I immediately felt her keel was stuck on something under the water and tried in vain to see it, I pulled on the oars and we scraped our bottom on whatever it was until it popped up in front of me and we were freed. The weighty bulk of dead sidekick bobbed up ominously. 'So, it was true,' I thought to myself, 'maybe he couldn't swim after all!' I took a puff on my imaginary pipe and headed back towards the top of the bay.

Once I got back to the car I headed straight for the motorway pulling off my beard, hair and jacket as I drove and throwing them in the passenger foot-well. The cricket coverage had started and I listened to the preamble as I put my foot down and headed home all the while checking my mirrors for signs of me being followed: there weren't any but I varied my route in any case. In just under two hours we'd taken two wickets but their leading batsman was heading for a double century. The familiar landmarks of home started to appear in front of me and I slowed down looking for signs that anything was different. I drove over the hill road and checked the gate I'd smashed and pretended to fix. To my surprise the farmer had already replaced the whole thing. The hedgerow had also been cutback which he must have done this morning or yesterday evening. As I entered the village I passed the tractor with its giant trimmers like swordfish snouts in their upright position. He waved, innocent of the fact it was I who smashed his fence. Or maybe he knew, maybe everyone knew? It was a small village after all, anything was possible.

At the bungalow I felt instantly from the gravel that I was the last vehicle to park there. I didn't know whether I was relieved or disappointed. If they weren't here where the hell were they? Jane's presence although welcome on one level had meant that I couldn't look for clues at James' house, or bash his brains in for information had it been him in the shower instead of her. I'd have to work on the assumption that the man who called me yesterday morning and the man who shot at me in the field and the men who took Peggy and the men I'd killed at the yacht club all knew me or thought they knew me from a former life. Or a supposed former life; that was the key. What level of need-to-know information did they have access to? I was still confident that they didn't really know anything but it raised the question of who Mr. Big was. I mean after all these years? Calling me in for what? Something they thought I had or something they thought only I could get? I was still sitting in the car when I heard and then saw the green and yellow cab of the tractor and its giant back wheels pass by in the rear-view mirror. I turned off the engine and got out.

Home, the familiar smell of the garden, and something a lot more pungent from the farm. I opened the front door and let the alarm go through all of its beeps before entering, stepping over the threshold just in time to neutralise it. Nothing untoward and no slobbery kisses from the dog whose odour was now mingling in my nostrils with the muck-spreading next door. I locked the door behind me and after gathering the extra kit I thought I might need realised I was hungry. I needed to think and food was going to fuel my brain as well as keep me going. In the kitchen I ate a ham and cheese sandwich with some of Peggy's mum's amazing marrow chutney, grabbed a bag of crisps and a cup of tea and then forced myself against my instincts to lie back in the reclining arm chair in the living room, close my eyes and meditate. I didn't even turn on the TV, just tried to focus on the birdsong outside and think back to how and when this had all started.

A song thrush repeated each of its calls as I thought back to yesterday morning and the phone call. 'I'm not darling I'm afraid,' vanity, someone who thought he was funny. 'And I think you know who this is and why we're calling.' Foreign and privately educated perhaps, and polite or was it just menace? No, of course I don't know who you are or why you are calling. What have you got to gain from these theatrics? Vanity again, you *like* the theatrics. 'How is retirement suiting you?' It was suiting me quite nicely thank you. You want me to know that you know I'm retired insinuating that we knew each other in the past or were acquainted in the past when I was still active. A slight hint of an accent, I'd say Eastern European or Greek originally. It could have been any one of a hundred known persons of interest but I did think he was probably about my age, which meant I bought into the whole we'd met before angle whether I wanted to or not. With a recording of the call I could have listened for background noise but I cleared my mind again and tried to pin down what had at first seemed familiar about the call. Bing bong. I was jolted out of my reverie. Who could possibly be calling the house at lunchtime on a Sunday? Not the postman.

The delivery driver handed me a weighty Jiffy bag that apparently didn't require a signature. I thanked him and went back inside to the kitchen. In my experience letter bombs weren't normally this bulky but I still boiled the kettle as a precaution and steamed open the flap before carefully checking there was no mechanism inside. Instead I found a man's hand wrapped in cling-film. 'James,' I thought. And he could still be alive, although I doubted it. I put the hand back in the bag and resealed it. If they'd killed James that might mean I was wrong about which side he was on or that he'd changed his mind trying to protect me perhaps? Either way I now had to worry about Jane's safety as well as my own family's and mine.

I found the gallery's phone number in my little black book and dialled. Jane picked up after four rings, her voice a little rough, 'Hello?' she said. She sounded nervous, scared.

'Jane are you OK? It's John from earlier. Any news of your dad?'

'I, I…please don't call me.' She hesitated before putting down the phone but did cut the call. 'Or the call was cut for her,' I thought.

What had I learned about my enemy? Ruthless, unpredictable…things weren't looking good for Peggy and Arthur but their captors knew that as soon as they laid a finger on either of them I wouldn't deliver. If I was right and they'd got to Jane too, that might be their first mistake – it told me they were still in that area, which made sense of course, and I got ready to jump back in the car. This time I booby trapped the bungalow and left with a bag of our shared personal effects expecting not to return.

Driving towards the sea for the second time I noticed the sun was lower in the sky and started to think about a day wasted. I rued the head start I'd so nonchalantly given them earlier. England were looking like snatching a draw from the jaws of defeat against all the odds. Of course that could easily change in a couple of balls either side of tea. When I got there Jane's door was ajar which didn't bode well. I ran up the stairs to find the flat turned upside down amidst evidence of a struggle. I ran my fingers through my hair in exasperation, the Browning still clutched in my right hand. What the hell were they playing at, and what did it mean for my next move? I felt like I was a good two steps off the pace now, and any confidence I'd had of being able to turn the odds in my favour had gone.

I searched the flat looking for clues but all I could find were signs of Jane and the bubbly girl who'd triggered an impulse in me: her makeshift pyjamas lying on the futon, the fag ends in the overflowing ashtray, coffee cups in the sink, Chanel no. 5 in the bathroom. The assailants had used force to get in, of that I had no doubt. If they'd already harmed or killed James I couldn't see the logic in coming for Jane? What was I missing? The cobbled street outside was busy now compared to earlier in the day and tourists were taking photographs and wondering aimlessly, languidly making their way to the beach, the fish and chips shop and the pub. The sounds of laughter and footsteps slapping on cobbles rang up the stairs from the open door as two or three kids ran past, and with the sun out it wasn't a bad Sunday afternoon for a stroll.

I checked the answer machine and listened to one new message, 'Hi Janey sweetheart, so sorry I missed you at the restaurant I'm such a useless trollop. I'll come round and make it up to you I promise, I've got to come to the shop anyway. Love you!' It was James' voice.

'But you didn't, did you?' I said out loud and saved the message. The machine confirmed my request with a loud beep. Three other saved messages. I listened back to them. The first was from James making arrangements for him and Jane to have dinner. 'Obsolete,' I thought to myself. The second call was a voice I didn't know but guessed it was from Mummy, 'Janey babes are you there? Be a good girl and give me a call please.' I would have automatically deleted it but stopped myself and pressed the button again. 'Hello?' It was my mysterious Greek. Of course it was. I don't think he'd meant to leave a message and hung up. It was another mistake. I listened back to the short message, barely two seconds long, to see if I could hear anything. Was I imagining it or did a dog

31

bark? 'Arthur, you clever bloody boy!!' I shouted at the phone and started to feel a million times better.

I felt that there might be a diary or notebook somewhere if I was lucky and had another rummage. On the only desk I looked at a gilt-framed photo of father and daughter outside what I assumed to be his house, the family home that I'd never been to. I needed the address and tried to see from the three shots in the triptych if I recognised the house or not. Rambling, red brick with a circular driveway and colonnades outside the front door, making our bungalow look tiny and insignificant by comparison. I looked for more photos in the drawers of the desk and in the bedroom but could only find holiday snaps. I stared probably too long at Jane on a beach in somewhere like Goa or Thailand, topless and tanned drinking coconut milk through a straw direct from the husk.

'Hurry up,' my little voice was telling me. I went to the kitchen again more in desperation than anything else and found two post-it notes under the calendar, one of which had a local landline written on it in bold biro. That had to be it.

I ran down the stairs just as the first honeyed rays of dusk hit the bamboo blinds and turned the brown apartment gold. Putting Jane's front door off the latch I pulled it shut as best I could in its broken state and pressed the Land Rover key fob. I got in and pulled up the collar of my body warmer, put on my driving shades and did a little wheel spin as I pulled out, at the same time checking all around for anything suspicious. England had had a minor collapse after tea and now had a nightwatchman in to protect the top-order batsmen.

CHAPTER FOUR

Reluctant to sleep in the safe house or the boat I checked in to one of the seaside hotels and decided to have a drink at the bar to see if I couldn't do a little digging. The hotel was a white art deco period property the other side of the bay on a slight rise. Surrounded by palm trees and the kind of hedges and lawns you'd expect to see on a links golf course in Scotland. Here, though, it was just the end of town and beyond it nothing but the vast Atlantic Ocean disappearing towards sunset and North America. All very romantic of course but on this occasion it would give me a good vantage point. I booked a single suite for a week (hoping it wouldn't take that long), paid for it in cash and went straight to the bar to catch the sunset. I'd also enquired about their private moorings and booked one so that I could bring the yacht here. As I sipped my gin and tonic on the veranda the pieces of the jigsaw started to come together and I was as confident as I could be that the hostages were all being held at James' house. Why he'd had to lose an arm, and probably his life in the process, I didn't yet know. I made it a habit never to take written notes but mentally I started to put all of the facts into little boxes so that they could be retrieved later. The sky was in the process of turning itself from scarlet and orange to magenta while the sea whispered secrets that only it knew to the rocks below me.

With one earpiece in I listened to the close of play and smiled as the nightwatchman hit a four off his legs from the last ball. Perhaps our luck was going to hold after all. I had a little transistor radio which I always used for

33

listening to the cricket on the move. I turned it off and put the earpiece back in my inside pocket. On my way to the room I stopped at reception and asked to see the local phone book to look up James' address. I was in luck, Parnell J., The Pines, High Road was listed with the landline I'd taken note of at the flat. I thanked the receptionist and wound my way up the carpeted stairway to my suite. I phoned reception and ordered prawn cocktail and a club sandwich from room service and helped myself to a half-bottle of white wine from the minibar fridge. While the food was being prepared I showered and shaved quickly and made a mental list of things to do tonight. It wasn't going to involve a lot of sleep. I dressed and ate with the cricket highlights playing on the TV and simultaneously studied the map. As I'd suspected High Road followed the coast and meant that The Pines could be accessed by sea as well as by land. I needed to get my boat, do a recce of The Pines, and put her into dock here. Then I'd need to take a drive and start trying to achieve-slash-retrieve the impossible which in many ways would involve me going back in time. The full moon was going to help me and I needed to take full advantage.

I wore black trainers with rubber soles so they could act as boat shoes, a three-quarter length wet suit, my shoulder holster and pistol, navy tracksuit bottoms, a black windproof jacket and Velcro fastened fingerless gloves. A black beanie would complete the look. A look I was just the right side of sixty-five to maybe get away with but there was no time for vanity I chuckled to myself and finished the second miniature bottle of white wine. Now all I had to do was slip out without them seeing me.

The suite I'd asked for was on the first floor towards the dunes side so it was relatively easy to climb out of my window and fingertip my way along to the edge of the wall and then drop down onto what I assumed to be the laundry room roof and out by the bins to the car park. There was a security camera on a tall pole in the far corner but its angle convinced me that I wouldn't be picked up until I got in and drove off. It was a risk I was prepared to take, at least I'd avoided having to speak to any nosey hotel staff on the way out. I now had the problem of where to leave the Land Rover once I'd got the boat? I couldn't leave it at the marina. I figured the mews' courtyard would be safe enough for a few hours. I looked at my watch – 08.30 p.m. – and decided to drive first, have a quick peek at The Pines on the way out, then go back in time and only ditch the car and pick up the boat on my return, towards dawn. I'd made a flask of coffee which I now put in the passenger foot well next to the pasties which I knew I'd be glad of in a couple of hours.

The Pines was only a few minutes out of town with a gateway leading to its private drive just off the main road. I couldn't very well just turn up, especially empty-handed but I needed to know what I was up against, and even whether they were all there or not. From studying the map earlier I knew that there was a coastal footpath which went past The Pines' garden and I could park in the public car park on the cliffs about half a mile beforehand. I found the turn and was relieved to see nobody else there, it looked like the sort of place lovers would come for trysts. I locked the Land Rover, grabbed my little black rucksack and set off at a steady trot towards the house. The moonlight shone silver on the sea and it was very beautiful, accompanied by the shrill calls of kittiwakes and terns and the flitting of the bats. Six minutes later I was there. I moved inland and crouched down to look at the house through binoculars once I'd got my breath back. As far as I could tell there was no sentry posted in the long garden but any closer inspection of the house was obscured by the synonymous pine trees. I entered the little wood and stopped to listen after a couple of metres. A tawny owl made a hunting call and I thought there was faint laughter from the house. I could also see lights now coming from the sea-facing windows. A closer inspection through the binoculars revealed that the curtains were drawn. I felt vulnerable and had little recourse to escape from this position if I was caught here. But I had to have proof that my hunch was correct.

I went as close as I dared and told myself that I'd go back from that position regardless. I lay down and held my breath, the smell of the leaves and pine needles in my nostrils and digging into my body despite the protection of the wetsuit. I heard a side gate open and footsteps crunching on gravel. A car started up and disappeared down the drive. Another noise, closer to my side of the house sounded like a dog's collar jangling. Could it be Arthur? I hadn't banked on him catching my scent but that could be disastrous, especially as the light breeze seemed to be coming inland from the sea which put me upwind of him. Arthur started barking and bolted towards me.

A voice called, 'Hey, what's got into you? Come back stupid dog! I only let you out to do your business. Come back here!' I imagined the man I'd shot in the copse yanking the lead and heard Arthur whimpering in submission. It was all the proof I needed. I waited for another minute until I was sure they were back inside the house and then made my way to the coast path and the Land Rover as quickly as possible. While I was jogging back another thought occurred to me; if they had captured Jane, which now seemed highly likely, and she had told them about my visit they could reasonably assume that I'd work out where they were. I had to hope it was a conversation they hadn't had.

I turned on the engine and took off my beanie. I also took off my jacket and holster to make myself more comfortable for the drive ahead. I hadn't turned the headlights on yet and was momentarily mesmerised by the moonlight on the sea below me. I drank a quick cup of coffee and ate half of one of the pasties. A cloud drifted across the moon and the night was briefly black again. Something made me turn off the engine and listen. I wound down my window and waited.

'Thwack!' I was vaguely aware of the car starting up again but it wasn't me driving this time. We drove quickly for a short distance and then I heard the tyres crunching to a halt on gravel. Somewhere at the back of my foggy brain I could hear a dog barking.

I came to hooded on a chair with my hands tied behind me and my feet bound together. My head hurt like hell and I was furious with myself for underestimating my enemy. I had new-found respect for their skills. 'Arthur,' I thought. 'It must have been the barking that alerted them.'

The hood was removed and a light shone in my face. I struggled to keep my eyes open against the glare and the pain seared through my eyeballs to the back of my brain.

A slightly Greek voice announced, 'I don't think you are taking your task seriously enough, John.' A sound

37

like a match striking and the smell of cigar smoke indicated that he was smoking. And then, 'You don't mind if I call you John?'

With my mouth still gaffer-taped I didn't think I was expected to join in the conversation. The man continued:

'Doubtless you have many questions. "Why me after all these years?" And "am I really the only person who can help you?"' He puffed on his cigar and exhaled. 'But it is only you who can answer these questions John. You must think!' He banged the table for effect.

The lamp was moved to a more congenial angle but the man talking to me was still in shadow. 'But enough of all this cloak and dagger nonsense, I expect you are tired and anxious to continue your journey.'

'Is this the voice of a man who cuts off hands?' I was thinking. And deep down in my guts I was terrified of what was coming next.

'For now your family are unharmed,' the man said quietly and then continued in measured tones, 'But please don't think I won't hesitate to kill them again if you persist in angering me. You have until six p.m. tonight.'

Part of my brain was still trying to place the voice and its peculiar use of English as the lamp was shone back in my eyes. Before I knew it, the cigar was ground into my face and I felt the red hot tip burning its way through my left cheek. I also caught a split second glance at the man's gold signet ring and bracelet. The smell of burnt flesh, cigar and gaffer tape mingled and filled the air. I screamed and writhed in agony but it was in relief as much as anything given that I had mentally prepared myself for much worse. And at least it wasn't my eyelids. The hood was replaced and with hands and feet still bound I was bundled back into the Land Rover and driven to the moonlit car park.

I must have slept because when I woke up the moon had waned and the horizon already hinted at dawn's first rays of light. My head and cheek were sore but a quick inspection in the rear-view mirror revealed a visage more rough than terminal. I had no choice but to go straight to the marina via the hideaway to leave the car and sail round the coast to the hotel. It was time to unlock those little memory boxes in the dovecote of my mind and start putting things together.

CHAPTER FIVE

It was 1970 when I finished my degree in Chemical Biology at Cambridge and came out with a first. I knew next to nothing about the world but probably too much about molecules and compounds and how to manufacture them. The weather was kind to us that summer and unusually for me I started being invited to social events like picnics and pub lunches and punting. Even the boat race against Oxford which a friend who owned a little MG had said he needed company on the drive to Henley for. There were evening drinks in college and dining at formal halls but I refused to attend anything as grand as a ball with all the proximity to females that that would entail. Petrified as I was of the fairer sex there were nonetheless one or two who kept cropping up. At first I quite liked a girl called Belle (short for Isabella), or at least I thought I liked her. We kissed once after a very awkward game of tennis while we were lying on the grass watching the cricket from a distance in the University Parks. Belle talked a lot in a sort of faux American accent – I learned later that she was half-Canadian. She said I was so intelligent that I could work for anybody I wanted and she, a physicist, was heading straight for London and insisted that I meet her friends to talk about all the job prospects there. She kissed me again and I imagined the molecules of her breasts pushing upwards towards me out of their flowery dress prison.

We met Belle's friends at a huge house near the sea in Norfolk. She drove us on another sweltering day in her little Lotus Elan which looked and drove like something straight out of a spy film. For driving gone was the flowery dress and in came the cut-off denim shorts. It would have been impossible not to be impressed, at least not for somebody who'd led such a sheltered existence as I had up to that point. Lunch was held outside and was for me the antithesis of everything comfortable in my life, confident good-looking people from the upper-middle classes and upper classes all talking excitedly about people they knew and jobs they already had lined up after the summer. 'Let's swim!!' said one. 'Let's swim naked!' shouted another. I almost broke out in a rash such were my palpitations and I would have been unaware of somebody whispering in my ear had it not been for Belle touching me lightly on the forearm to get my attention.

'I find all of this a bit much, don't you, old boy?' The broad smile revealed rows of glittering white teeth but slightly pink Polaroids masked what the eyes might otherwise have told me. 'Come inside and let's have a quiet cup of tea.' It wasn't a request despite the convivial body language and I stood up, leaving my napkin on my plate. 'Don't worry, Belle here knows how to look after herself! Don't you, old girl?' He laughed a hearty laugh and squeezed her shoulder before putting his arm around mine and leading us through the veranda doors into the main house. Everything was immediately cooler and silence reigned supreme as if we'd gone back in time to the days of the Raj. And that's how it all started, in the study of a Norfolk country house I was recruited to the Secret Service.

Soon after and quite by chance I met Peggy. Of all the things now being drummed into me as part of my training for my new double life, learning how to cook wasn't one of them. I'm a sandwich man at heart anyway,

41

and Peggy worked at my local café. I think I thought at the time she was the owner but in fact she was an employee, just the girl who made the sandwiches. It didn't matter. I loved the sandwiches and I loved Peggy. Every Monday to Friday morning Peggy would have my sandwiches ready in a brown paper bag for me to collect as I cycled past on my way to the train station. Cheese and tomato, ham and tomato, cheese and ham, ham and pickle, it didn't really matter as long as Peggy had made them. No egg mayonnaise that was my only rule. If I finished work in London early enough I would also pop in for supper on my way home. Peggy didn't always work that shift but I enjoyed the hot food and of course it meant I didn't have to cook. The café was normally busy at weekends but I always made a point of going in at least once to have a full English breakfast, Peggy's were always the best, and do the crossword.

'What do you do in London?' she asked me one day, picking up my plate and pushing her hair back behind her ear. A sign, I now knew, that she liked me.

'I'm a scientist.' That was one of my permitted answers and as a white lie could stand up to the court of a relationship or even a marriage. I was and still am a scientist. It's just that I also became something else in the process. And something that I helped to create and protect was now coming back to haunt me.

We started dating in a slightly old-fashioned sense for 1970s England which was all down to the fact that I'd never had a proper girlfriend. Peggy was more streetwise than me and thanks to some of the boyfriends she'd had before me I think she appreciated my quietness. Or rather how quiet she thought I was. I liked the fact that she knew more about this stuff than I did and that she liked boys and wasn't shy to say it. I was ready for her to teach me all she knew. It was a welcome change from the sometimes dreary shinning up ropes and lumping over obstacle courses. I'd rather climb all over Peggy after a long hot day in London or a cold wet day in London or at least tiptoe towards the outer edges of her lower slopes while we sipped Guinness and she smoked roll-ups and we made each other laugh. We'd go to the cinema or cycle along the river or visit museums and see who could do the best sketches of the naked statues. It was all very natural and innocent and, I now realise, very romantic.

Once the Service had vetted Peggy and said everything was OK we were married in a small East Anglian church called St. Peter's. Our honeymoon was in Athens, I was working of course but for Peggy it was our honeymoon and nine months later Karen came along. Two years after that Karen had a baby brother called Will but things were difficult for him from the beginning. Ultimately we lost our little bundle of joy when he was barely one month old and it was awful for all of us. That's when we got a puppy (the one two before Arthur) whom we foolishly called Will which only meant that when he passed away we had to grieve all over again for our lost baby. It's not something you ever get over, the loss of a child, and it changed the dynamic of our marriage as well as our relationship with Karen. She eventually emigrated to Australia and we hardly ever see her. I suppose now with the wisdom of hindsight I would say that Peggy and I didn't talk about it enough. We didn't discuss what we were actually feeling with each other and bit by bit it drove a Will-sized wedge between us. There was, and still is, love. Just that the silences are always filled with that unspoken thing which is a terribly British, and terribly ineffective way, of dealing with something.

Athens wasn't the only foreign posting. There was Argentina, Kuwait, Cuba and Angola plus dozens of European trips which were so short that I didn't need to take the family with me; the likes of Brussels, Helsinki, Copenhagen and Paris. All on a diplomatic passport under an assumed name, naturally. I only killed when I had to but it was sometimes, and increasingly became necessary. In my regular debriefing sessions they taught me how to build emotional and psychological layers which would enable me to deal with almost any situation without emotion. I might display pain but I wasn't feeling it.

We didn't always live in the retirement bungalow, before that we had a large Georgian terrace house in Cambridge, three storeys plus attic and basement, a house full of spider plants and cacti and art. It was gorgeous and more than we could ever have dreamed of probably but when we lost Will even the house took on an almost spectral guise. Day-to-day we did all the things; me getting the train to London, us travelling the world, Karen becoming a woman falling in love and starting her own life. Peggy still worked in the café and loved it, she also enjoyed going out with the girls, the new keep-fit craze and getting her hair done. We had a good sex life and had fun in all the rooms, except Will's room.

In my circle or cell there were very few constant faces but I was now forced to recall each one and analyse which of them had been capable of treading the path to treason they'd now set foot on. The Greek, as I'd pigeon-holed him, was familiar but I couldn't yet remember where from. Certainly he wasn't someone I saw in the lab or the shooting range or at the OPS HQ we had at an active RAF air-base on a daily basis. Only four of us spent all of my Service years together in that lab; me, Mike, Carole, and Panayota (Yota for short) and I felt that I knew them, knew their motivations and personalities inside out. Mike the proud and committed patriot who'd gone on to do great things and quietly risen to dizzy heights in the Department since I retired. Carole whose parents had come to England from Jamaica on HMS Windrush in 1948 had been in the Service since the 1960s and ended up in the lab after long stints in every other department. She may have wanted to be an operative when she first joined up but her fighting spirit was long gone, just happy to have a job that got her out of the house. I knew less about Yota but liked her, she was young and like me had been brought in because she was just too good at chemistry. Something of a genius with test tubes and microscopes and pretty with it, her ancestry may well have been Greek but I don't remember meeting any acquaintances or family members. Again I felt certain that Yota was not grinding any axes, or if she was what could it possibly be that it would wait twenty-five years before bubbling to the surface?

In the field I operated alone with a handler and it would be no easy task to recall every mission and filter through each and every contact I'd made. Might there be enemies? Undoubtedly, but most known enemies had already been dealt with.

The two-pence-coin-sized hole in my face was irksome but there was little I could do about it other than try to keep it clean. This I did with the car first aid kit before driving back into town and the boat club. I changed my mind about going back to the hideout and left the Land Rover at the hotel before jumping down to the beach

45

and walking in the direction of the marina. There was nobody about at dawn barring one or two fishermen and the usual sea gulls. The waves grabbing and dragging great handfuls of shingle from the shore seemed to be saying 'rush, rush' and I quickened my pace.

No more incident tape or police car at the harbour master's office and I walked quickly along the wooden walkway to my berth. I primed the engines and made sure they both had fuel before turning the key. They burst into life and bubbled happily under the surface, the blue slick of diesel and the fumes lingering over the green sea. I cast off fore and aft and jumped back on board to deftly turn us away from the boardwalk upright and out towards open water. Following the buoys I sped through the chop to the hotel. It only took ten minutes but gave me the adrenaline rush I needed to kick-start this important day. I went straight from the dock to the dining room where as I'd hoped I was alone at the breakfast buffet. Though not the first person to eat I noticed as there was one dirty place setting with discarded napkin and up-turned coffee cup. I filled my tray and ate quickly in the corner of the room by a lace-curtained window which gave me a good view of the sea. I spotted the day's newspapers laid out next to the fruit station and grabbed one, scanning the headlines and the obituaries out of habit before turning to the cricket. The nightwatchman took all the plaudits.

Fifteen years out of the Service meant that all high-level access privileges had been revoked. There was nowhere I could simply walk into and demand to look at files or start conducting experiments. What the Greek wanted had been developed completely by accident in 1969 by an Italian called Nardi, long since dead. His obituary wouldn't have been in *The Times* but his death would definitely have been talked about in certain circles and indeed it was part of my job to carry on his work. I started looking at the crosswords but knew there was no time. I'd take the paper with me and look later if I got the chance. What was it the Greek had said? I sipped the last of my second cup of coffee and gulped another grapefruit juice. 'Only you have the answers. Think.'

Was I about to mount a daylight raid on a secure facility? No, I didn't think it was plausible, not without dying. And my capture last night put paid to any thoughts of a raid under darkness. I was running out of time and options. I thought about the signet ring and the bracelet, the cigars and the formal English. 'How is retirement treating you?' I grabbed a banana on my way up to the room. 'It's not darling I'm afraid.'

I needed to ditch my cat burglar outfit in favour of a more respectable retired senior civil servant's attire. I turned on the radio and the shower. Why now? Because the Greek had a buyer. Why me? Because since Nardi died I was the only person who could make it. As I fiddled with the complimentary shower gel and turned down the hot water a tad I thought 'if a daylight raid to steal something is out of the question, what about a daytime raid to make something?' But I'd need a proper lab. I had some equipment hidden on the yacht but not enough to safely build anything unstable with. Then there was the humanitarian question. I hadn't worked my whole life protecting democracy to go and give a deadly chemical weapon to the first criminal-type who threatens my family. I turned off the shower and wrapped a towel round my waist in order to shave. Somehow I was going to have to circumnavigate my wound with a razor blade and find a way of making it look less ghoulish. Was I still capable of creating something with an almost identical chemical signature but that would be far less deadly? I thought I could probably do it given several months. I had no idea whether or not I could do it in a couple of hours. A sticking plaster to cover my wound and a bit of hotel hair gel completed the fresh look.

I was going to have to do something I hadn't done for years and get the train to London. First I gathered what scientific equipment I had in the yacht and put it into my specially modified Gladstone bag. I would also have to go unarmed if my academic cover was going to hold water so I hid the pistol on board and locked up the hatch again. My watch said 08:22 a.m. My heart beat faster as I wished for a few more hours and I knew I was really up against it now. I drove as fast as I could to the nearest mainline commuter hop-on point and paid for all-day parking. The next train to London would arrive in twelve minutes' time which was just long enough for me to buy a coffee and start looking again at the paper. Going back to the obituaries I started to read about a prominent Greek scholar who had dedicated her whole life to the return of the Elgin marbles to Greece from the British Museum. The platform got more and more crowded as late commuters and day-trippers appeared seemingly from nowhere. Expensive fold-up bicycles were the order of the day for the cyclists which seemed a long way from being helped on board the guard's van with my heavy bike in the good old days. When the train arrived I found a seat and tried to settle and straighten my thoughts. For the lab work I was going to have to have some sort of theoretical strategy prepared given the timeframe and I started to mentally scribble formulae in my mind. Specifically this information had not been brought down from its boxes for many years and as I watched it float around and coalesce I was filled with premonition about what could go wrong if it fell into the wrong hands. Or even what might go wrong if I messed it up and killed everybody in London.

I still had one or two friends or old spies as we called ourselves and I rang Mike from the train explaining in veiled terms that I needed urgent clearance to visit Nightingale, our lab off Hanover Square, today.

'Erm sure John, let me see what I can do. What are you working on? Everything OK?'

'I'm fine thanks Mike, it's just a personal project that grew beyond the potting shed, and I happened to be in town.'

'I should be able to get you into your old office. I can't see you as a gardener.'

'Well it certainly beats fly fishing.' Beats fly fishing was a code word for help from the past. I hoped Mike would remember and if he did, hoped he'd have time to meet me at the lab. I settled into my seat and started to look at the crossword.

CHAPTER SIX

Jane was damned if she was going to be held prisoner in her own home and due partly to the fact that her initial remonstrations had been met with such force (she could still feel the bruises), coupled with the fact she had a deep-felt foreboding that her father was dead she would be quiet for now. They were all held in the same room and the clock chimed nine a.m. The smell in the air indicated that it was time for the dog to go out for his twice daily exercise. In fact, she thought, the dog was being treated much better than they were. She and the other woman had hardly spoken since Jane had spent her first few hours recovering from being beaten into silence after her initial outburst.

'What the fuck?' Jane had woken up feeling better but dehydrated and in need of a fag. She stared at the other woman and her smelly dog. 'Who the fuck are you anyway? Any why the fuck are you here with your dog, in my house?' Jane sat up with some effort and winced.

'Maybe you should take it easy for a while longer,' Peggy said concernedly. 'They gave you quite a beating.'

'It wasn't they, it was that bastard the Greek guy. And I don't think it was the first time he's hit a woman. Fucking sadist.' She stood up and paced around the room, opening the curtains to see who was outside and shaking the handle of the locked door. 'Come on you bastards it's time to let this dog out and I need to use the loo as well!!' She banged on the door. There was no immediate response but they could hear sounds and voices in the house beyond the room they were held in.

'They're coming,' Jane said satisfied.

'My name's Peggy and this is Arthur,' said Peggy. 'And I don't know why we're being held here.'

'No offence,' said Jane, 'but I really don't care what his fucking name is.' She pointed at Arthur who looked suitably offended. 'Are you famous? Is your husband rich? Who's being held to ransom here?'

'It's OK baby,' Peggy said ruffling Arthur's ears, then to Jane, 'If you'd asked me who my husband was any time before two days ago I would have said he was a quiet, law abiding civil servant. Then out of the blue there are guns, car chases and kidnappings. The one thing I do know is he will come and get us. Don't underestimate my John. You said it was your house, right? Maybe you can shed some light on our kidnapping?'

Jane sighed and exhaled through her nose, her shoulders drooping in resignation. She sat next to Peggy and said, 'Look, all I know is that my dad disappeared two days ago and then these thugs came to my flat and captured me.'

'I feel like I don't know anything anymore,' Peggy put her face in her hands and started to cry.

'I know, me too,' Jane put her arm round Peggy's shoulders and stared abjectly out of the window.

Arthur went straight to the door as if he'd heard something the ladies couldn't. Suddenly there was the sound of the key unlocking the door and as the guard opened it inwards Arthur made a bolt straight for the back garden wagging his tail as he bounced down the corridor, through the kitchen and outside.

Jane was quickly to her feet and said to the guard in a tone that wouldn't take no for an answer, 'I'm coming out as well! You can't keep us locked in that bloody room forever!' Before he could say anything she turned left and locked herself in the little downstairs loo for a much needed pee. Jane heard noises outside as one of the cars started up and left. She washed and dried her hands and noticed in the mirror how badly the man's rings had cut her cheek and eye. 'Bastard,' she said to herself and in that moment vowed revenge. She came out of the bathroom with a changed countenance, flirty and dangerous.

'Where's he off to, your boss? I'm starved let's make breakfast.' She headed for the kitchen. 'Cup of tea anyone?' Jane had assayed the pecking order correctly and it was clear that without their ring-leader the guards were going to be a pushover. 'Let Peggy out as well then, you idiot. Please,' she flicked her fingers in the direction of the corridor and ordered the guard to go and unlock the study door. 'Good boy, and when you've done that I'll be in the garden having a fag, OK?'

Moments later Peggy appeared outside the kitchen door with her hand held up to shield her eyes from the sun, 'Arthur, come here baby!' she called. There was a reassuring rustle from the wood and a snarl which suggested Arthur had found something to stick his nose into. 'Don't eat any poo you naughty boy!! Arthur come back here!!'

'Must you shout like that, it's very disconcerting?' Jane was doing her best to relax and enjoy the sea view.

52

She sipped her tea and simultaneously took a drag from her cigarette, 'I made you a tea, it's on the side, did you see it?'

'Arthur, good boy, come on!' Peggy crouched low enough to slap both palms on her thighs while Jane rolled her eyes, behind her shades, which she must have picked up in the kitchen Peggy thought. With the dog back in sight Peggy fetched her tea and sat down next to Jane, 'It's a lovely house,' she paused to look around, 'what does your father do? I mean could he raise a million pounds to spring your release?'

Jane didn't take offence, 'Daddy? *God* no!! Don't judge us by The Pines, it's his inheritance, and mine too hopefully if we all live long enough.' She shook her head and stubbed out the cigarette, 'God, I'm starving aren't you?'

'Yes, we should try and keep our strength up,' she said as they went back into the kitchen. Arthur bounded in waggling his whole body and tail in search of a bowl of water which Jane was rather uncharacteristically Peggy thought now pouring, 'There you go whatever your name is,' Jane patted Arthur and put the dog bowl outside.

'I'll make breakfast, you go and keep an eye on the dog and our captors,' Jane was clearly in control of her emotions this morning and Peggy felt bad for having judged her.

Arthur now had half a garden's worth of gorse and bracken attached to the hairs under his tummy and Peggy set to work untangling the mess but was also alert to her surroundings. John her husband of more years than she cared to mention had left her alone day after day to take the train and work in London. Yes there had been trips abroad but there had also been long weekends and hours of Peggy-alone or Peggy-alone-with-the-kids time and Peggy was no fool, she had long suspected that the Civil Service scientist job might be more than it appeared but had never said anything. She was proud that John was a spy or an agent or whatever it was, he deserved it, and that's why when it all kicked off she'd made love to him like she had when they first met and she was still working at the café. Put simply he was the man she loved most and despite all that they'd been through she wanted him to know that she was always there, now just as always. Peggy had done her own research; what skills might the wife of a government agent need? And quietly she had acquired them – observation, secrecy, discretion, self-defence, obfuscation. Now, it seemed, she would put them to good use or die.

Arthur had finished drinking water and ran off towards the front of the property, the bit that Peggy was not familiar with, at least not in daylight, and she duly followed suit. After the gravelled access alleyway they emerged into the car park but to the left there was another path leading to a clapboard style garage that appeared to have accommodation above it. Arthur kept going resisting any attempt by Peggy to inspire his return. To Peggy's surprise there was another armed guard at the garage house, visible through the downstairs window but apparently oblivious to what was going on outside with what looked like a portable TV for company.

The grassy path petered out in a wall of thick bushes and trees and Peggy dreaded trying to get Arthur back through all the brambles. The gables of a second house which looked as if it was definitely on the same property were visible through the branches but Peggy couldn't readily work out how it would have been accessed, or maybe it was just abandoned she thought?

'Arthur, come on!! Here boy, come on!!' After what seemed like an age Arthur came back looking forlorn and covered in even more thorny branches. 'What happened to you, silly dog?' Peggy scolded outwardly but inside she felt relieved that he had at least tired himself out a bit. Peggy put his collar on and dragged him unwillingly back to the main house where the smells of cooked breakfast made Arthur undergo a miraculous recovery.

'Good walk?' Jane enquired on their return, and was busy plating up bacon, eggs, sausage and tomato. The smell of toast as it popped up from the toaster mingled with the aroma of filter coffee and music played on the radio. 'That would be the cricket,' Peggy thought, 'If John was here.'

'Come on let's eat outside,' Jane said conspiratorially, 'I've got a plan.'

Peggy groaned inaudibly dubious about Jane's ability to plan anything clever enough to get them out of this predicament but she was hungry and genuinely impressed that Jane had cooked. The food was good and very welcome and Arthur behaved impeccably as all dogs do when they know they're going to get titbits thrown at them from the table.

'Thank you for this, I'm very grateful,' Peggy said. 'Where's our armed escort?'

'Upstairs on the phone to his girlfriend,' Jane replied, 'I overheard them talking dirty to each other.' She stabbed a sausage and held it up for inspection on her fork, 'Unfortunately,' and she bit the end off, smiling.

'Arthur ran round to the left over there by the garages,' Peggy said waving her knife in that direction, and she took a bite of toast and marmalade before sipping her coffee. 'I followed him and saw another guard at the garage. What do you think that means? And who lives in the overgrown house over there?'

Jane put her knife and fork together and reached for her cigarettes, 'Do you mind if I…?'

'Go ahead,' Peggy lied. Although this experience was making her turn a lot of her world view on its head, and she was young once too many lifetimes ago.

'Let me check out the guard situation, there is a sort of pied-a-terre up there above the garage. Maybe they've got Daddy there! God, Peggy you're a genius! The other house is a *long* story but rest assured there's nothing going on there, believe me…' she smoked wistfully and seemed in no hurry to check out the garage.

'So what was your plan?' Peggy had also finished and gave what she had deliberately left for him to Arthur who lapped it all up in one gulp and then looked like he needed a nap. She missed John but didn't expect Jane to understand.

'I've called the police,' Jane whispered with her head down and eyes peering at Peggy over the top of her sunglasses.

There was now an awkward silence. Jane continued to smile in a way that invited approbation but Peggy demurred, 'Bloody hell, you did what? My husband's got until 06:00 p.m. tonight to deliver what they want or they'll start killing us. Don't you understand that? If the police get involved these guys are bound to get upset and we're dead for sure and probably John as well!'

'Well how was I supposed to know all that? Calling the police when the guards are distracted seems to me like something any normal kidnapped person would do, don't you think?' Jane started to sulk and lit another cigarette.

'You're probably right but we're not talking about normal people here, or common criminals for that matter. I say let the spies handle it.' Peggy had the upper hand again and was going to use the momentum to do what she instinctively felt would protect them, 'What do you know about the sea round here?' She stood up to look out at the coast over the long garden. 'Would escaping over the clifftops be better than going by road? We need to start thinking about ways out of here before the shooting starts. But first let's find out who or what is being protected over there in the garage.' Jane's shoulders had slumped and she didn't offer any answers. 'I'll do the dishes,' said Peggy, 'Here, pass me those plates please.'

Their idyll was abruptly shattered by the crunch on gravel of the boss coming back. The errant guard reappeared from nowhere and brutally shepherded them all including Arthur back into the study and locked the door. They could hear the clattering of dishes and the sound of running water as the guard frantically tried to clear up their breakfast. Perhaps he would say he'd cooked

57

it for him and the other guard. Jane stood at the window and pulled the curtain towards her slightly to get a look at their tormentor. In the daylight he looked older than she'd thought when he laid into her from the shadows but he might have been attractive in his youth, she supposed. Not good looking exactly but swarthy and wealthy with a hint of danger. He had brooding eyes which offset his ugly demeanour.

The Greek (they still didn't know his name) slammed the door of his Mercedes and came through the front door shouting, 'Hey what's that smell? I'm starving! I hope you guys saved some for me.' Then as he joined the guard in the kitchen they could no longer hear what was being discussed.

Peggy sat back on the sofa and stroked Arthur, 'Reckon you can pick this lock?' she raised her eyes towards Jane who was still peering out of the window.

'No, the locks are pretty solid I tried as a kid. The sash windows on the other hand…they really are child's play,' she grinned back at Peggy.

'Right,' said Peggy, 'we need to formulate a plan and a contingency plan for the most likely outcome. What time is it?' It was a rhetorical question as she looked at her watch. 'Nearly 11:00 a.m. That gives us seven hours to get ready.'

'Ready for what?' Jane asked.

'One way or another this thing's going to be decided tonight. Tell me what you said to the police.'

Jane sat cross-legged on the floor but objected to having Arthur's wet mouth on her leg, pushing him away. 'To be honest I don't know if they even heard me. I dialled 999 and got through to the police but reception was bad and the call cut as I was giving the address.'

'What did you say was happening? Kidnapping?'

'No, I didn't get that far. I'd said missing persons because of Daddy.'

'Sure,' Peggy paused, 'don't worry Jane I'm sure there'll be some sort of explanation soon enough.'

'Yeah, but it may not be the one we want.' She started playing with Arthur's ears. 'What do you think we should do?'

'You know the area better than me. There must be a paper and pen somewhere in here?' She said looking around.

'Yes, here.' Jane got up and found one in the desk.

'So you think about escape routes; a) for us three, b) for us plus your dad and my John, and c) just for you. John will have a plan in mind no doubt but you'll still know the property much better than him.'

'It's whichever way isn't blocked,' Jane said quickly. 'I mean with a car out the front is fast assuming the lane to the main road is clear. If not, assuming we have a boat, the sea might be a possibility.'

'Do you and your dad have a boat here?' Peggy asked.

'No,' Jane shook her head.

'Any idea what time high tide is tonight?' Peggy was taking notes. Something John never did, she remembered.

'Again, no idea.'

'So,' Peggy extrapolated, 'the sea's only good if John comes with a boat and the tide is favourable.'

'What if your husband gives them what they want and they let us go?'

'Then we just go free.'

'And the police? If they follow up my 999 call?'

'If they follow up a missing persons call and come here we'll either be executed or the kidnappers will be spooked and it might play in our favour, if they panic I mean. One of two ways.'

Jane was beginning to think that the John who visited her yesterday morning was probably Peggy's husband but something was keeping her from telling Peggy. She didn't really know why she didn't want to say anything but for now it was her secret.

There was a long silence broken by Peggy, 'Let's keep an eye on that curtain and if the guard from the garage comes here that will be our chance to creep out and see what's going on over there. I mean it's a risk but...'

'I'll do it,' Jane volunteered, 'I'll be faster and the dog won't make a fuss if I go. Plus he's my dad and I have to know if he's still alive.'

CHAPTER SEVEN

Crossing London on the underground and by foot wasn't quite the same as cycling all those years ago it but I still got a big homecoming thrill that only the capital can bring. Each of the famous landmarks held memories for me just as they did and had done for millions of people over the years; the Strand, the Embankment, Tower Bridge, London Bridge, Oxford Street, Marble Arch. I nestled into the tube and put my leather briefcase on my lap, hugging it with my arms and careful not to look anybody in the eye. I used my peripheral vision to make sure nobody was watching me and felt confident that I was just another bowler-hatted man on just another packed tube train.

London isn't a clean city but in fine weather the trees and parks with their blossom and flowers lend it a kind of borrowed cleanliness and everybody forgets the grime for a few hours. It was one of those days as I walked the last little bit of my journey to Hanover Square and stood in front of an unmarked door. If Mike had pulled the right strings the door would open of its own accord, no need for me to knock or ring the bell. I simply took off my hat and stared at the invisible camera. After what seemed like an eternity the door opened wide, silently, and a middle-aged Sri Lankan lady took my coat, if she recognised me her features didn't reveal anything. Not even a flicker of recognition despite my enthusiastic smile, perhaps she was trained not to recognise old spies and only greet the active agents. A broad shouldered armed guard stood with his feet apart and hands clasped together just below the belt buckle in the shadows behind her. He ushered me towards a double-thickness glass security door and took my bag which would go through the scanner separately on a conveyor belt. The front door had long since closed behind us. No words had yet been spoken. I waited for the red light to turn green and the click of the door lock which would allow me into the foyer of the building I had known intimately for many years in a previous life. It now felt that perhaps my loyalties had been misplaced or at least I had been mistaken in thinking that my love for it was reciprocated. The light turned green and I stepped through to be reunited with by Gladstone bag.

'John, it's been too long. What can I help you with?' Mike appeared as if by magic and shook my hand. He did that thing important people do by placing his left hand on top of our hand shake.

'Likewise Mike,' I smiled. As we made eye contact I realised that I was trusting someone outside the family against my instincts but felt I had no one else to turn to. 'Did you secure a lab?'

'Please follow me.' Mike nodded at reception as if to say "It's OK, he's with me" and we walked the polished granite corridor to a lift that we'd shared many times before. Neither of us said anything until we'd reached our destination deep below the streets of London and he had swiped us back into our old lab.

'Is it safe to talk here?' I asked looking round furtively but there were no other scientists in evidence.

'Yes it's fine John, no one's listening. What sort of trouble are you in?'

63

'It's personal, at least for now. And I'd like to keep it that way if I can…' Then I expanded. 'My family's in danger, Mike. I need full access to the lab just for a couple of hours please.'

'I've cleared the lab until tomorrow, that's fine. Why don't you call it in? Have you thought about that? We can help…Obviously if the national interests are compromised given what you know…' He didn't appear to be pressurising me it was all very casual and I felt he was as awkward as I was toeing the party line.

'No, not yet, Mike' then thinking on my feet, 'But you can monitor the situation by all means, that's fine, and I'll be the first to give the go-ahead if I can't complete.' I knew that Mike would assign a drone to me as a matter of course but condoning it made me feel better plus it would be good to know that I had the option of military strike power in the event of things going terribly awry.

Mike made notes in a tablet he was carrying while I put on a white lab coat and goggles, washed and scrubbed my hands and donned gloves before taking out various vials from my Gladstone bag.

'Right, I think I'll leave you to it,' Mike said and started for the exit.

I pulled down my face mask and said matter-of-factly, 'I need any intel. you've got on a Greek public school type, gold signet ring, gold bracelet, speaks good, slightly old-fashioned English with a sadistic streak a mile wide.'

Mike looked at my cheek and said, 'Cigar smoker?'

'As a matter of fact, yes,' I said and went back to my microscope. I flicked on my trusty transistor radio to listen to the cricket and discovered that the nightwatchman had fallen just before the mid-session interval. Not exactly a heroic match winning contribution but he'd put the tail in a position to survive until lunch and England looked like declaring, up against it timewise and praying for clear skies to get a bowl at the visitors. I was in a similar situation timewise but instead of eating cucumber sandwiches at Lord's I was tucking into another Cornish pastie in subterranean Mayfair. I looked at my watch – it was already mid-day – and knew realistically I didn't have more than a two-hour window to complete my task and get out. I hunkered down and focussed on the task in hand. Re-creating the virus from the control we'd created all those years ago kept under lock and key in a near-identical but less lethal way. Ninety minutes later I thought I had a placebo version which would fool a non-expert for long enough to free my family. What they'd then do to me having found out it wasn't going to wipe out a whole village or city neighbourhood would then become my prime concern, of that I had no doubt but we'd be far away on *Oystercatcher* by then. Under the microscope, Type II looked identical and had many of the same physical characteristics as Type I but this one was only going to give you a bad cold with flu-like symptoms rather than knock out your entire nervous system and shut down your visceral organs. I wasn't prone to day-dreaming but with the cricket on in the background and my task almost complete I sensed a very foggy memory of having met the mysterious Greek before. I was reminded that he claimed to know me and wondered what kind of lunatic he really was, prepared to chop off limbs and kidnap a retired scientist's family in order to get his hands on a terrifying biological weapon?

A buzzer and a light went on and I was shaken out of my trance as Mike appeared at the lab's Plexiglas window. He held up his omnipresent tablet and mouthed, 'I've got something for you!'

'Hang on,' I replied. First I had to make everything safe for him to enter. I got up from my microscope and started to put the deadly virus back in its secure vault. At least I hoped I wasn't about to give the wrong virus to the wrong man, or the right virus to the wrong man, or the wrong virus to the right man, or even the right virus to the right man. Whichever way I said it in my head it didn't come out right. I smiled at the word play and turned off the cricket.

'Sorry John, I didn't mean to startle you. I've got some info.' He put the tablet down on the work surface between us and started to explain. 'We've got an intercept from the emergency services switchboard of an incomplete missing person's report but when they traced the line back it came from an address called The Pines, mean anything to you?'

As I stared Mike in the eye my gaze gave nothing away and I wondered deep down how much of a friend he really was? My years in the Service had taught me to trust no one and I couldn't help thinking that securing the lab had been a bit too easy. Why? Were they interested in me or already interested in the man I called The Greek and his gang? Could I have made the fake virus anywhere else I asked myself? No was the answer, I'd had no alternative. I didn't want Mike's heavies to get involved and trample all over the place and possibly get Peggy and Jane and Arthur killed in the process. My gut said say nothing but I knew Mike would see through a blatant lie and want to know straight away why I wasn't letting him in on it, 'Yes,' I said, 'there's a girl whose father is somehow involved in all this, I think. A friend of a friend, she said her dad was missing. Maybe she called?' Nothing about that's where they're holding my wife, where I'm going to hand over the merchandise and start killing terrorists on my own if I have to.

Mike returned my gaze and seemed to understand that there was more at stake here than simply doing an old friend a favour but that the time for all that wasn't quite yet, 'OK John, we'll look into it. Should I tell the local police to follow it up?'

'Wow,' I thought, 'so Mike already has surveillance in place,' this guy is good. And dangerous I didn't doubt. Keeping him at arm's length was going to be difficult. 'Yes,' I said glibly, 'I can't see why not.' I could see a million reasons why not but anything that riled the kidnappers might not be such a bad thing.

Mike pressed his tablet screen and swiped it a couple of times and then continued, 'I put the description you gave me through the computer and came up with one most likely candidate. A guy called Demetri; he was a bit of a local hero in the 1970s, cult political leader. History of violence though and hasn't been active for a long time, or at least hasn't done anything to get back into the spotlight, until now. Can't be much younger than us John.' Mike met my eyes with a smile as fake as it was wide. 'What do you think he wants?'

'Well we know what he wants,' I said patting my satchel. 'What we don't know is why he wants it.'

We walked out and rode the lift together so that I wouldn't have any trouble clearing security. We said our goodbyes and I was reunited with the overcoat I clearly wasn't going to need. 'Oh,' Mike turned and very casually asked, 'did you get what you came for?' From where we'd sat in the lab I could see there were at least four surveillance cameras on us and I knew he already knew the answer to that one.

I smiled and waved behind me as I stepped out into the sun, shirtsleeves rolled up, jacket in one hand and briefcase in the other.

CHAPTER EIGHT

The noise of breakfast being prepared and eaten continued from the kitchen for a while, followed by the smell of cigars and cigarettes being smoked. Arthur was sulking on the carpet with his head lying on one side, no one smoked at home and he didn't really like it. Plus he wanted to be out in that big garden again chasing pheasants in the woods. Jane and Peggy had both tried to get some sleep since their first plan-of-action chat and they were dozing when they heard the unmistakable sound of footsteps approaching their window. They were right next to the front door of The Pines so it could have been the door that was the destination as well. Maybe the guard from the garage had come to the main house for a break? For a split second neither woman breathed and even the dog seemed to hold its breath. Jane made the tiniest gap between the curtain and the glass and caught a glimpse of grey shorts which of course told her it was the postwoman.

'False alarm,' Jane said out loud.

'Postman?' Peggy asked.

'Postwoman, actually,' corrected Jane.

They all went back to napping and subconsciously counting down the hours and were woken up by the sound of a vehicle driving in from the lane and pulling up to a halt on the gravel. This time Peggy opened the curtain a tiny bit and could plainly see that it was the police.

'Is it the police?' Jane asked.

69

'Yes,' Peggy whispered. Arthur started whimpering and it was clear he wanted to bark. The 'ding-dong' of the doorbell seemed to shake the whole house which had suddenly become very quiet. Peggy and Jane's heart rates went through the roof as they listened to the Greek and his guards running round frantically trying to think of how to play it. The door to the study burst open almost inaudibly and the Greek and one of his men came in and violently grabbed Peggy and Jane in headlocks with one hand over their mouths. Arthur was livid but the guard threw a cushion on top of his head and knelt on it while he held Peggy's neck and clamped her mouth. There was a crackle from the police radio outside, 'Tango two-four come in. What is your loc. Please?' It was so loud, that it sounded as if it was in the room with them.

'Tango two-four receiving, I am at The Pines responding to a possible missing persons 999 call, over.' The female officer responded.

'Copy that Tango two-four, once you're done we've got reports of a domestic abuse incident involving a known offender on Hamilton Avenue please respond. Over.'

The radio faded abruptly as if the PC responding had turned the volume down. Neither Peggy, Jane nor their captors had heard a second officer talking but surely there must be one Peggy thought? Otherwise these guys might cut their losses and kill only one officer for getting in the way. 'Bing-bong,' the doorbell rang again and this time the PC knocked on the front door's glass as well. 'Hello, anybody there? This is the police.' From inside there was only (muffled) silence.

The female police officer looked through the letterbox and tried to peek through the study curtains before going down the side alley to look round the back. In the study there was much scuffling and wriggling, especially from Arthur who almost got himself free. Peggy was convinced the dog would die if the criminal's weight wasn't lifted soon and she swore her own pact of vengeance should fate grant her the chance to exact it. Before long the radio crackle was back and they heard the police car start up and leave.

Just as Jane was thinking, 'My God, these police are dumb,' the Greek let go his strangle hold and started shouting, 'Right, I want to know who called the police? This is a very dangerous game and could have caused many deaths!' He was pacing the carpet and clearly furious.

Peggy and Arthur were also released but it took Arthur a few seconds to come round properly and gain the strength to get up and snarl at the guard. He was just about to go for him when the Greek unlocked the door and said, 'It's OK, let the dog out.' Arthur ran out to the garden to contemplate his mortality.

Peggy was furious and replied, 'Don't you think calling the police is a perfectly reasonable thing to do if you've been kidnapped?' She made as if she was going to indignantly follow Arthur but the muscle man grabbed her arm. 'Let go of me you swine! That poor animal was almost killed by you just now,' she brushed his arm aside and went out into the corridor.

'Follow her,' the Greek nodded, and then turned his attention to Jane. 'What about you?' She was still kneeling below him and he grabbed her lower jaw bone with his right hand, pulling Jane's lips into an awkward pout and thrusting her head back, 'Have you been busy on the telephone?'

He let go and she collapsed in a heap briefly before regaining her composure, 'Where's my father? Why are we being held here?'

'Take a seat please, let me tell you a story.' The Greek sat on the chair by the desk and let Jane settle on the sofa, he held a brass letter opener shaped like a knife point-down on the old-fashioned blotting pad beneath the tip of his right middle finger and span it round repeatedly. Jane noticed that the index finger next to it was crooked and realised that it must have been shortened in an accident at some point. 'Your father used to work for me, but he made a mistake. And now he's being punished.'

'That's not much of a story. And I don't believe you.' Jane stared at him angrily.

'Come, let's join the others outside, I suspect we'd both like a smoke.'

Jane led the way and they all ended up sitting at the slatted garden furniture on the back terrace. They could smell the sea and hear the distant roar of the surf on the beach below the cliffs, it was a beautiful day. After they'd both lit up the Greek repeated his question to Jane, 'Did you dial 999? Tell me the truth.'

'No, I didn't. It could have been anybody local, Daddy knows a lot of people round here.' Fear had forced Jane to lie and she denied everything. Peggy was impressed for the second time that day. 'Do you mind if I use the bathroom?' Jane stood up and stubbed out her cigarette.

'The downstairs bathroom, yes go ahead.'

Upstairs had been out of bounds since their incarceration began and Jane still didn't know why. But that wasn't her priority right now. Right now she locked herself in the little downstairs loo, turned on the radio and noticed it was tuned to the cricket. She had some vague notion there was probably a test match being played somewhere. She turned up the volume and then used her gymnastic agility to crawl out of the top slit window. She'd done it as a girl to break in whenever one of them had lost their front door key but as a grown woman it was slightly more problematic yet she managed and hunched over double ran as quietly and as quickly as possible to the far garage. Avoiding the front windows through which Peggy had seen the guard watching TV, she went round the back and had to crawl through thick brambles and nettles to get there, to reach the fire escape on the other side which was the alternative access to the upstairs bedsit. Knowing that she had no time to waste she tiptoed straight to the top and tried the little glass-panelled door. It creaked open and then a gust of wind slammed it into the staircase banister and she held her breath. No sound other than a desktop fan whirring and rotating slowly. Her eyes took a second to adjust to the darkness of the room but although it was years since she'd been up there she could recall the layout. Somebody was prone on the bed at the far side underneath a mosquito net and being kept cool by the fan.

'Daddy, is that you?' Jane whispered and crept close enough to make out that he was also attached to a life support machine and a drip. 'Christ, what have they done to you?' There was a noise and it sounded like the guard was about to come upstairs, 'Shit, I've got to go, love you Daddy.' Jane crept out the same way as quickly

73

and quietly as she could, this time ducking underneath the windows in the front of the garage to avoid the thorn bushes at the back. Then it was a tiptoe sprint across the gravel to the bathroom window and the contortionist act in reverse to get back in. The guard was banging on the door and shouting, 'You OK in there? I'm going to bust this thing down if you don't hurry up!'

Jane flushed the loo, twice, ran both taps and splashed water on her face. She turned off the radio, shut the window and unlocked the door, looking down her nose at him and saying, 'What's the big fuss? You've obviously never been married, right?' Jane was about to head straight back to the kitchen and garden but the guard used the barrel of his gun to direct her back to the study. The three of them were locked in again. As the door clicked shut she shouted through it, 'What about some lunch? We're hungry and thirsty in here, you know? Hey, come back!!' It was more for show than out of real hunger.

'Wow that was brave, well done. What did you find out?' Peggy indicated that Jane should join her on the sofa and made Arthur shuffle up on the floor so that they'd have enough room.

'They're holding Daddy here, you were right. I have no idea why! None of this makes any sense. He's alive but they've hurt him. God, it's all so awful.'

'Maybe my John isn't the only man with a secret life in this whole mess.'

Jane wondered how much else Peggy didn't know about John and thought he looked too young to be her husband. Perhaps he'd just aged better, 'If the police come

74

again before the deadline I'm going to raise the alarm, I'm sorry but my dad needs to get to a hospital and these bastards need to be stopped.'

Peggy thought for a second and then said, 'Yes, I agree. That's another contingency we need to put on our list.'

'Fuck your list!' Jane shouted back then she said, 'Look, I'm sorry, it's just really annoying that's all, must you be so bloody practical about everything?' She got up and rattled the door handle again, 'where's our fucking lunch?' This time she meant it and even Arthur was scared.

CHAPTER NINE

Just after 04:00 p.m. while I was still on the train back from London listening to the cricket and willing the locomotive to go faster, I received a telephone call.

'You have less than two hours left. Do you have what I asked for?' The Greek's by now familiar voice sounded less relaxed for some reason, I wondered if they'd had a visit from the police. I thought about Mike handing me Demetri's identity.

'Indeed, I do. Are your guests all still in one piece?' I was on the train after all and maintaining politeness. At Lord's they had just broken for tea which made me think maybe the caller was also listening to the cricket? That hazy memory still refusing to coalesce. I thought of India, tigers, Rangoon. But nothing concrete.

'They are,' Demetri replied and I felt he was thinking on the hoof which was good and played to my strengths, 'do you know the Waterfront Hotel?' he asked.

'Yes, I do,' indeed I did. He'd bowled his googly but I'd spotted it and hit it down off my pads. Of course he wanted to meet somewhere public and my assumption this whole time that we'd do the handover at The Pines was now blown out of the water but I was already familiar with his apparently random choice of venue. Would he risk bringing his hostages to a public place? He might if they were becoming a liability.

'We'll meet in the bar at 06:00 p.m. on the dot. Don't be late, and come alone.' He hung up. I got the feeling that this Goliath had lost his will to fight or had the air knocked out of his lungs. He'd bounce back of that I had no doubt but this moment of insecurity or introspection, or whatever it was might be all it took to get the girls back and get out of there alive.

By the time I got off the train and started driving back towards the hotel it was gone five and fast approaching six o'clock. I had to believe that they didn't know I was staying at The Waterfront already or that I knew about The Pines, that they still believed I had no idea where I was taken blindfolded in the car that night. The Pines was my trump card. If Demetri failed to deliver the hostages as agreed I would have to go and get them. With no time to sail round the coast in advance I could only play it by ear but be as prepared as possible for every eventuality. I was anxious to retrieve my favourite Browning from the boat before our rendezvous although I had a back-up in the room and one in the car come to think of it. I also wanted to change into something less formal and restrictive.

05:42 p.m. I forced myself to relax and did all of my tasks with eight minutes to spare. I settled at my usual table on the terrace with one eye on the sea and the visible bit of the car park and one eye on the door of the hotel. I looked like a weekend sailor on shore-leave, cotton jacket over short sleeved shirt, cotton slacks and deck shoes, the shoulder holster not visible to the untrained eye of any other hotel guests or staff. I sipped gin and tonic with bitters and fresh pink grapefruit, apparently it was on special that night and it was bloody good, I thought. At 05:58 p.m. there were two simultaneous roars, one from a

77

powerboat cutting its engines to glide into the private dock and one from a large SUV with tinted windows that pulled into the car park. Subtle it was not. Through my sunglasses and the brim of my straw hat I counted four men, two on the boat and two in the car, plus their ringleader. No sign of the girls or Arthur but they could easily be in either vehicle out of sight. Only two men made their way towards the bar, Demetri and one of his henchmen. Both men armed I deduced by the single-buttoning of lightweight jackets not dissimilar to my own. The sunset started to soften the glare of the day's sun and there were sounds of laughter from other guests also enjoying today's happy hour cocktail.

They walked straight over to my table and sat down. I half stood up and sat down again for appearance's sake but there were no handshakes, just grimaces that would have passed for smiles from a distance. I called for the waiter with a raised arm and resisted the temptation to order another G & T while the thugs ordered a beer each. The three men left behind all stood like bouncers on nightclub duty, two guarding the speedboat and one guarding the car. All very mafia-like and conspicuous, but I suppose it wasn't too much to imagine that a wealthy guest was having a drink at the hotel.

The drinks arrived and first sips were taken. Demetri sat opposite me with his back to the sea and the sun which meant I couldn't really see his features clearly a bit like when he'd hidden behind the shade of the lamp. I half expected his right fist to break my cheekbone or grind a cigar into it again.

'You don't remember me do you?' He said, cutting straight to the chase.

78

'I don't I'm afraid,' I said, unable to lie for the sake of it. He shook his head from side to side in disappointment and drank some more beer, which was fast finishing I noticed. 'I need to see that my wife is alive.' As I said it I expected a door or a cabin hatch to be opened so that I could see them inside but instead the bodyguard sitting to my left put a mobile phone on the table which was playing a live video feed of Peggy and Arthur in confinement. I picked up the device and watched my wife on the screen, 'Hi Peggy love are you OK? Did they hurt you?' I asked, then added, 'where are you?' for effect.

'We're fine John, darling. Don't try and come here, darling, they're expecting you!' Then the call was cut and the screen went black.

'Hand it over. And don't try anything or you will all be killed.'

'I have questions,' I said, and immediately wished I hadn't because it weakened my position. Both men stood up and forced me to also stand and hand over the small black fanny pack that I'd put Type II in. Anybody watching wouldn't have seen anything untoward and for the first time I wondered how much of this was being filmed from on high by Mike's drone.

'If everything is correct you will receive your packages in twelve hours' time. Good day.' Demetri produced a handful of money from his pocket and left a twenty pound note on the table, placing it under his glass.

As soon as Demetri and his entourage had turned their backs heading for the exit and the car park I pocketed the banknote thinking that he'd been careless to hand me a fingerprint. But then I could have taken one from the glass as well if I was that desperate, I supposed. At any rate I'd put the drinks on my room and it wouldn't matter. The speedboat crew had been slow to notice that their boss was leaving, and that simple act made me formulate a plan bolstered by the sound of Demetri's SUV putting itself into first gear to accelerate up the steep hill onto the cliff road. As fast as I could I headed in the boat crew's direction and discreetly drew my gun. With the silencer attached I should be far enough away from the bar not to draw too much attention to myself and besides I was acting purely on instinct rather than worrying about the consequences. If I could take out one or both of these guys or even just disable their boat I'd increase my chances of rescuing Peggy and Jane (and Arthur of course). I was shooting into the setting sun but I still got the man nearest me before he could even reach his gun. He fell into the water and was dead I was quite certain of that. The second bodyguard fired at me but I ducked and he missed, my second shot from prone hit him in the face and he fell back into their boat. I ran over to squeeze one more shot and finish him off. A tad melodramatic perhaps but I knew that these guys were not going to let me live once they realised that the virus I'd handed over wasn't deadly. I found a boathook and lifted the body of the first guard onto the boat and dumped him on top of his friend. Then I untied their stern line and ran, or rather speed walked to attract less attention, ten yards further along the boardwalk to *Oystercatcher* and untied her as I jumped aboard. Within seconds we were cast off and underway. I put the yacht into reverse and attached the speedboat's bow to my stern so that I could tow them out to sea with me. Then with one hand on the wheel I glanced back at the hotel terrace through my binoculars but there was no great flurry of activity much to my relief. I'd got away with it, for now at least.

As I sailed out into deeper water I couldn't help feeling bitter about the deaths I'd caused but the training I'd had all those years ago had drilled into me that it was either them or you and remorse, certainly during a mission, could be a fatal flaw. I put my engines to idle and went below for some plastic explosives and a timer. I looked at my watch and anticipated at what time I could use a diversion later on and set the fuse for one hour from now. That would give the sky time to get dark and me time to get back to the little copse at the side of The Pines. I dropped the speedboat's anchor, laid the explosives and carried on my way. There was a moderate swell with a handful of white horses but once again we were blessed with a stunning sunset. From studying the lay of the land on my last visit I knew that there was a small private bay with anchorage where I would leave the yacht and hopefully return the same way with Peggy, Arthur and Jane. I drifted into position, dropped anchor and tied us up fore and aft. It occurred to me that Demetri would soon start to wonder where his men and his boat were and I hoped I'd arrive before he'd had a chance to dish out any retribution on the girls. It had never crossed my mind that I would wait until six a.m. tomorrow on the off chance that they believed the virus' fake chemical signature and handed over the hostages.

While I waited for it to get a little bit darker I re-checked all my equipment and changed into my black assault outfit. I also called Mike and told him to send the local police in about an hour and a half, with an ambulance. The ambulance was for James who, if he was still alive, would definitely need one. The Department's boys should wait for my signal which would be a green flare once my family was safe, or in the event of my death storm the house immediately, whichever came first. Mike reluctantly agreed. For this battle I'd also blackened my face and felt pretty ready as I crossed the sandy bay and started to climb straight up the sheer cliff-face. There was a tarmac path but I couldn't run the risk of bumping into anyone, although I would definitely use it coming back, for speed. Sunset was in its last throes dyeing the cirrus clouds in the sky above the hotel a blood red and closer to me as I climbed, bats and owls were out hunting and dive-bombing past my head, or at least that's what it felt like. The sound of the waves crashing on the beach got further away until I reached the top and after looking both ways ran across the path in a crouch position and got my breath back in the woods.

Climbing up from the cliff I'd arrived at the western edge of The Pines on the opposite side to my last visit. To make my attack from here might be disorientating but more importantly I hadn't recce'd it and didn't know if I could even get through to the main house. At first glance the undergrowth looked a lot thicker than the woods side where Arthur had smelled me last time, and before long he'd be scenting me again I thought. The one thing that could be said in favour of coming this way was that it gave me the element of surprise and was bound to be less well guarded. I decided to go for it and if nothing else it would give me a better picture of the complete site.

Through the branches I could make out the lights of the kitchen through the conservatory doors and from here it all looked very cosy and calm. I knew that Demetri would be executing his get-out plan now that his hideout was compromised and he had his biological weapon.

That's what I'd do if I was him. I might be too late. I ran forward as quietly as I could and came to what appeared to be an abandoned house on the same property. A thick wall of brambles meant I couldn't go any further, at least not without using a torch to find a path. 'Shit,' I cursed my luck. Just then a door opened at the back of the house flooding the long garden with light and simultaneously I could hear Arthur barking in what I felt certain was delight. 'Shut up, Arthur,' I thought to myself, 'not yet, boy. Not yet!'

'What's he barking at?' Demetri was quickly onto the dog's abnormal behaviour.

'It's the badgers, sir. I saw two running away when the light came on.'

The light had in fact given me an option to move forward over the barbed wire fence surrounding the outlying property and onto its overgrown driveway which was at least grass and not thorns. In no time at all I came to a two-storey garage building and from here I could see the main house and the cars parked outside it on the gravel forecourt. At the garage I stopped underneath a fire escape which ran up the outside of the building and listened intently. At first I thought I heard voices but then realised it was a television, I decided to move on. Whatever was happening in this building was happening sedately. The main house was a different story I crouched under a window on the right hand side of the front door with my back to the bricks and almost immediately recognised both Peggy's and Jane's voices coming from the room opposite on the left-hand side of the front door.

I still had surprise on my side and if I used enough speed now I might be able to get the women out before we made any contact and more people died. If James was being held here I couldn't take him on the boat injured as he was anyway. I skipped across the front door keeping as low as possible and listened at the window of the room I now assumed was being used to keep the hostages in. No sound of a guard's voice, plus it didn't make any sense to keep a man inside the room, so I tapped on the window and whispered 'Peggy, it's me.' Almost immediately the curtain moved away from the glass and Peggy signalled that she understood. A second later I saw Jane pull up the sash window and climb out. She hunkered down next to me and I felt a frisson of excitement, as if we were about to kiss or hug but Peggy's arrival soon put paid to that and grinning, we moved off in different directions. Peggy went right towards the alleyway and the garden presumably to get Arthur and Jane went left the way I'd come, presumably to get her father, who I now realised must be in the garage I'd passed.

'Peggy!' I hissed loud enough that Jane could also hear me, and I frantically beckoned both women to come back.

We crouched together as close to the wall as possible and I took charge, 'I came by boat and we go back as one unit via the coastal path to the bay below the cliffs, understood?'

'I'm not leaving here without Arthur,' said Peggy.

And simultaneously Jane said, 'I'm not leaving here without Daddy!'

84

'Arthur is no problem we'll whistle for him once we clear the property and are on the cliff path. Jane your dad needs a doctor and he can't come with us on the boat, I'm sorry. I've already called for an ambulance.' I looked at the sixty-minute countdown on my watch, nine minutes left. 'Which way is quickest back to the sea?' I asked.

'Definitely this way,' Peggy said remembering the thorns and pointed towards the alley and the wood, 'I'll go and get Arthur and meet you on the cliff path. Besides, Jane will need help with the armed guard once you get to the garage.' It was brave of Peggy and I could see she'd made up her mind but I knew instinctively that splitting-up at that point was fraught with danger.

'OK love,' I kissed her on the lips, 'stay low and move quietly, Arthur will come as soon as he smells you. Here, take this.' And then, 'Be careful the safety's already off.' I thrust a pistol into her hand and she headed off without further ado.

Jane squeezed my hand and said, 'Come on.' Before I had time to remonstrate she disappeared into the darkness and made me feel very old. I could hear distant sirens wailing and wondered if the police had disobeyed my instructions or whether Mike had overruled them. Either way in about six minutes' time all hell was going to break loose at The Pines. When I got to the garage I couldn't see Jane until I heard a noise at the top of the outside staircase and realised she'd entered the building, presumably to say farewell to James. I noticed that the downstairs door was ajar and peered in before pushing it along its runner to open it a bit wider and squeeze through. At exactly that moment a hand came crashing down from the inside and knocked my gun onto the floor.

I was inside and facing a man twice my height and half my age. Dressed in boxers and a vest he didn't appear to be armed but he was alert for a man who had just been caught napping. I went low and swept my leg to take out his left ankle and unbalance him. At the same time I grabbed my Browning and fired into his chest. The big man clutched the entry wound in his chest with both hands and slid to the floor with his back to the wall. I turned on my head torch and located the stairs, running up to look for Jane with my pistol held out in front of me in case there were any other guards. I found Jane kissing a very frail James on the forehead. He was lying in bed under a mosquito net and by the looks of things was hooked up to a drip and a life-support machine.

'Let's go,' I said gently, turning off my torch. I went outside to the top of the wrought-iron steps, 'Stay close and let me lead, OK?' And then I added, 'don't worry it's all going to be fine.'

Jane nuzzled into me and whispered in my ear, 'Yes, let's get these bastards!'

The guard I'd shot had found enough strength to block our escape at the bottom of the stairs and demanded to know, 'Who the hell are you?' before he squeezed off a couple of shots. He was too weak and his aim was wild. I put one more into his chest and pulled Jane's hand behind me. There was now shouting and barking from the back of the main house and lights were being switched on all over the place. The overgrown path to the abandoned house wasn't lit and we ran down it to the fence and the edge of the cliff path. From here it was the metalled boat ramp to the bottom and freedom. We climbed over the fence and 'BOOM!' our eyes were drawn seaward where a giant ball of flame rose up into the air like an erupting volcano as the speedboat went up in flames.

The police car sirens were much louder now and I surmised they were practically on the driveway. We heard shots being fired in the garden and I knew I had to help. I turned to Jane, 'Go down to the boat and wait for us. Here's the ignition key and my torch, you can raise the anchor and start the engines. Go!'

'OK boss,' Jane grinned. 'Don't get killed,' she said and kissed me on the cheek before running down the hill towards the harbour.

I ran up the cliff path towards the end of the garden and was met almost immediately by a bounding Arthur who leapt up to greet me. Next Peggy came into view but I could see she was injured. She collapsed into my arms, 'Thanks for the gun,' she said, 'I got the one who nearly killed Arthur.'

'Are you shot? Oh Jesus, Peggy, this is all my fault I'm so sorry love.' I cradled her and stroked her hair, smiling into her eyes.

'It's not your fault, darling, you're my hero. I'll be fine.' She summoned enough strength to meet my eye contact and squeeze my hand.

Then we heard the police officers' voices and saw their torch beams trying to make sense of the situation and tend to the wounded. I suspected that Demetri had long gone, probably by car about the time I first heard the sirens. The flames at sea had receded but still lit up part of the sky like a late sunset.

'Come on Peggy, love, let's get you to the boat.'

'You go, John. I'll wait for the ambulance.'

'No Peggy, they'll interrogate you. These men can get to you in a hospital!'

'You are the love of my life, Johnny,' she squeezed my hand harder and drew me closer. 'Thank you for a good life, you were a good husband.' Arthur joined our embrace as I kissed Peggy and felt her last breath.

PART TWO

CHAPTER TEN

Jane had done her job well managing to weigh anchor and start the engines which bubbled in neutral, *Oystercatcher* bobbing gently in the swell. Soon the tide would be ebbing and this bay would no longer be any good.

'Hi,' Jane said hugging me and stroking Arthur as we got on board, 'Where's Peggy?'

'Peggy didn't make it,' I said simply. 'And the Greek's gone, you can go and be with your Pa now.' I don't think I realised how brutal I was being.

'And what if I want to stay with you?' Jane looked up at me with her pretty cheeks and green eyes shining in the afterglow of the fire and the moonlight.

'It's not fair, Jane. Not now. Believe me, I'm sorry.' I held her close and for a second she rested her head on my shoulder. 'I'll come for you, we'll see each other again I promise but right now you need to be with your dad and help the police. It's no use both of us becoming fugitives.'

'I'm sorry about Peggy,' Jane said as she climbed off the boat, 'Bye Arthur, I did grow to like you a teeny bit!' And she peered through a gap between her left thumb and index finger to emphasise the joke. Arthur wagged his tail and put his front paws up on the jackstay, sad to see her leave.

'Please untie us at the bow,' I said and watched the lights of the police torches coming closer down the path. I could also see that a group had already gathered by Peggy's body. I smiled and waved as Jane did so, the right words just weren't coming.

Jane set off up the hill at a run and I put both engines to full ahead. I was racing against the tide plus I wanted to put as much distance as possible between me and the events in my life these past forty-eight hours. With the speed and the wind in our faces it was hard to distinguish the tears from the salt water spray. Once we hit the deeper open water, I cut the engines to put up sail and headed south-south-west. My sat. phone started to light up and vibrate:

'That was quite a show you put on for us, John.' It was Mike. 'I'm sorry about Peggy, by the way. That's harsh. She was a good lady.' I didn't say anything. 'Any chance you can come in to be debriefed? There are one or two people here who want your head on a platter, and mine for that matter!'

Mike knew I wouldn't come in he was just doing his job and might very well be in trouble for helping me. 'Do me a favour, Mike?' I asked. His turn to be silent and not answer, 'Make sure Peggy gets a good send off?'

'Sure, John, we'll take care of it.' Then, 'You can't go after him on your own you know?'

'Why not, he's made it very personal now?'

'We also have an interest in catching him, John.' Did he mean the Department or him personally?

'Then let me help you. Fax me the file.' I said authoritatively.

'I'll send what I can, give me the number.'

Just like the lab in London, I thought, it all felt all a bit too easy. I gave him the number. Finally Mike asked, 'How are you going to disappear with the whole Secret Service tracking you?'

'Ha ha,' I laughed, 'that's my business. Goodbye Mike and thanks for looking after Peggy.'

I thought Mike might have been at The Pines personally watching us from the clifftops but judging by the noise coming from the fax machine he was still in the office. I checked on Arthur who had found his dog's nest and was curled up asleep. I thought about Peggy, about the good old days – the cigarettes and the sandwiches, teaching me how to be with a woman. All those years she'd known but never said anything and when it came down to the wire she'd proven her loyalty by dying rather than give in to the evil forces I chased for a living. Fighting for a cause she'd supposedly known nothing about for the past twenty-five years. She'd proven herself a hero and now I felt angry, with myself, with Demetri, with the world. Why couldn't I have just sat and watched cricket last Saturday afternoon while my wife walked the dog? But then I might never have met Jane, and that first glimpse of her in the flat was forever etched into my memory.

I had provisions on board for four people for a minimum period of two weeks. With just me and the dog these could be stretched to a month if need be but Mike was right, it would be some trick to disappear from the satellite view mid ocean. I didn't buy Mike's angle that I was suddenly public enemy number one and the Department was throwing all its resources into hunting me down. I had a feeling it was more personal with him, just a hunch but I think it suited Mike to have me as a retired operative surreptitiously going about his personal business. What business it was of Mike's I didn't yet know but I wanted to find out. I think he'd called me to make sure I was alive, to tell me off for being so bloody public and lastly to make sure he knew where I was heading. Was he distancing himself? Was it damage limitation? Maybe there never was any drone or satellite cover if Mike was flying solo on this one?

I spread out my charts of the English Channel, the Bay of Biscay and the Mediterranean. There was only one place Demetri was going – he was heading home and that meant Greece. Averaging six knots we'd make the 2400 nautical miles to Greece in seventeen days.

I slept with the autotiller on while the fax machine continued to click away quietly. I woke up in one of the world's busiest shipping lanes – the English Channel – with myriad passenger ferries, oil tankers, shipping container ship and yachts like me all vying to criss-cross each other safely and get to or from or through or round Europe. The sea was choppy and we were still under sail, I had the main sail up and the jib. We were doing six knots and had quite a good heel on but the heavy traffic and the swell made me think about bringing the jib in or switching to engines soon.

A grey coast-guard cutter, more than twice my size, appeared from nowhere and hailed me by loudspeaker. 'Ahoy there *Oystercatcher*, this is the Royal Navy. We are doing routine checks in this channel and request permission to come along side.'

Could I be wrong? Were the authorities going to bring me in so quickly after all? I prepared myself mentally to face the music and take my punishment. At least now I would be able to attend Peggy's funeral.

I signalled with my arms that permission was granted and proceeded to bring down the sails and reduce my speed as the giant cruiser came along side. 'Permission to come aboard?' They boomed. Several pairs of hands then threw ropes and caught ropes and jumped on deck. It was all terribly civilised and terribly fast.

The petty officer introduced himself and reiterated that it was just routine, 'Where are you heading sir?'

'Italy,' I said, which was true, 'my wife passed away and it's a holiday for me and the dog,' which was not entirely true.

'Yes, he's a handsome fellow.' Arthur had come up to see who all the visitors were. 'How are his sea legs?'

'He's not sure yet,' I smiled.

'We'll need to see your papers and insurance please. One of my officers can accompany you below decks.'

'Of course,' I replied. We went below and I produced the right documents from their file.

'You can go up sir, thank you. Please show this file to my captain. We need to conduct a quick search for contraband or stowaways, I'm sure you understand.'

I did as I was told. And I did understand, but I didn't understand why *Oystercatcher* wasn't on their wanted list, and why I wasn't being detained. Five minutes later and it was all over. Had the officers remembered to search me they might have wondered why I had a semi-automatic pistol and a confidential government file tucked into my trousers.

CHAPTER ELEVEN

'Demetri was from a remote village in the mountains of central Greece,' I read. 'Growing up in the 1960s he and his brother endured a four mile walk to school, both of them barefoot, his older brother carrying him through the winter months. The priest at the monastery which served as the school would have to thaw them out before any teaching could begin. They were shepherds from a poor, hardy community. Opportunities were few and the Greek economy was in bad shape. Demetri did well at school but his older brother didn't have the aptitude and fell into a life of crime while Demetri continued to read books. The young academic became interested in politics and activism and devoured the news of student demonstrations sweeping the globe whenever they went down into the village to get supplies. He came to idolise his older brother who was already getting into trouble with the police by the age of fourteen. Now too big to be carried the two still walked to the monastery and back together and they talked about escaping: escaping the mountains and the village and the poverty. His brother wanted to free himself but Demetri wanted to free his people. The mountain families like them were famous for not wearing shoes, it was a badge of honour, but born out of poverty more than a desire to have hardened soles. With the priest Demetri talked about philosophy and religion and cricket. The monks had a team, high in the Pindus Mountains and taught him and the other local boys to play with them. With his father he talked about sheep, about when to sheer them, about lambing, about when to go to market and what to barter for when he got there. With his mother he

95

talked about how to make cheese from sheep's milk and how he mustn't be like his brother and how he must use his education to get away from here and have a better life. There were, of course, one or two girls in the community but they were schooled at home by the grandmas and kept more or less under lock and key. They caught glimpses only at church and on the saints' days and other festivals when the whole village ate together in the little square.

Hard work took him all the way to university in Athens where he studied politics and law. Greece was still in the vicelike grip of The Colonels and the university was a hotbed of activism. Personal life – Very little is known about Demetri's personal life. It is thought that he never married and doesn't have any children that we know of.'

Either we knew very little about this man or the information was need-to-know only, I thought. Still I absorbed the background that Mike had sent and filed it away mentally. With the girls on board I would have sailed straight to the isles of Scilly or the Channel Islands or even west coast of Ireland, somewhere we could hole up and not be found while the dust settled. As it was I had decided to sail straight for Greece via the Bay of Biscay and Gibraltar. It would have been much quicker to fly, obviously, but this way I didn't have to pass any potentially tricky airport customs and immigration checks, and when Demetri realised he wasn't in possession of one of the world's deadliest biological weapons he wouldn't be able to find me. Plus whatever evil scheme he was hatching could not take place now given that I'd sabotaged its most potent aspect.

The next day we had much calmer weather as we sailed down the west coast of France and into the Bay of

Biscay and Arthur and I both sat on the deck listening to the cricket via the world service on longwave. Now that it looked like we weren't being hounded by the authorities we were going to have to enjoy the cruise. I wished that I'd let Jane come and realised that I missed her, and of course I was very sad about Peggy.

With no crew on board there was more than enough to do to keep the boat sailing, and being this physically active was quite a healthy way to grieve; silent and meditative but focussed on staying afloat with no time for negative introspection. The food wasn't up to much but while we still had fresh bread it was sandwiches for me and it would be dog food or dog biscuits throughout for Arthur. For the first week I couldn't even face tinned food but soups and baked beans, tuna and sweetcorn inevitably infiltrated their way into the dinner ranks to supplement my diet of bread and pasta. The fruit I'd stockpiled lasted a week as well before I indulged in canned peach slices and condensed milk. It seemed almost criminal to pass so many places famous for their decadence – Cap Ferret, Biarritz, Bordeaux – eating dried rations. Somewhere off the coast of Vigo we shared a solemn moment in memory of Peggy while Mike reported that the private ceremony had gone well. We pushed on through Spain and Portugal but as we entered the Mediterranean I scheduled a stop at Gibraltar. Here we could stretch our legs and re-provision ahead of the next leg to Sicily. Arthur, or was it me, was getting maudlin without female company.

Sliding, as many have done before us, between Mount Sidi Musa on Morocco's northern tip and the thousand foot high granite of Gibraltar's rock we couldn't help but feel slightly heroic. Arthur was also suitably impressed by the white monolith rising up out of the sea and the hundreds of cargo tanker ships and oil tankers going about their business of bunkering between oceans. We, as part of the slightly more modest yachting fraternity, made our way to the Gibraltar Point yacht club, got permission to dock and made our way to shore with relief.

Shopping could wait until tomorrow as we treated ourselves to fresh seafood and fresh bread and salad. I had a gin and tonic before drinking two large glasses of white wine. It was all rather romantic and after so many days at sea, mostly with no alcohol, I dined with both Peggy and Jane in my thoughts and chastised myself for the mistakes and errors of judgment on my part which meant we weren't all together now. A bit tired and very hungry I hadn't wanted to walk all the way into town yet, and had allowed myself to be lured in by the restaurant closest to the marina. As I ordered coffee and thought that I should probably let Arthur stretch his legs before bedtime, I noticed that the man reading his newspaper in sunglasses who had been there on our arrival was still there and still wearing his sunglasses.

I ordered the bill and paid and we strolled along ground that didn't yield or fight back and we were both a little wobbly. I remembered to buy an English newspaper from one of the newsstands but also bought a local paper in case it had anything interesting in it that hadn't made the international press. In a mirror amongst the postcards where tourists could look at themselves trying on sunglasses I saw our companion also pay his bill and set out on an evening stroll.

As he headed in our direction my heart rate started to quicken and I dragged Arthur reluctantly back towards *Oystercatcher* where at least I'd be armed if it came down to a fight. A moped engine roared up behind me making a noise like a bee and sped off up the road out of the harbour. The unidentified man from the restaurant took the same turning and I felt my muscles relax. A week at sea had left me out of sorts and jumpy. I decided that I needed to go for a run and as soon as the dog was asleep I slipped out and ran as hard as I dared, heading straight up the famous rock hoping that the equally famous Barbary macaques would be asleep. For the time of night there were more people about than I would have expected in England and the strolling couples and other joggers were protected by armed police patrolling in pairs. I stopped halfway up and gasped for breath and felt the rain of macaques pooing and peeing on me from the branches above. I carried on to the top, feeling the burn of lactic acid in my thighs from all the steps, and witnessed the moon rising out of the sea once I'd warmed down and finally felt relaxed enough to watch it. Much of my frustration had dissipated and my body hadn't let me down which was a relief. I knew I was feeling the effects of grief and probably fatigue as well if I was honest but I was tough and I determined to stop giving myself such a hard time. I jogged back down once my sweat started to chill in the night air.

Back on board having showered and changed my clothes, I made a pot of coffee and started to re-read Demetri's file. By now I'd read it a number of times and I felt I knew him reasonably well. It was perhaps too easy to romanticise poverty but the barefoot childhood in the mountains sounded adventurous and idyllic. I understood the excitement of Athens in the 1970s because I'd also been there, but again that's not to gloss over the hardships experienced by many ordinary Greeks under the Generals. I didn't know where our paths had crossed but it didn't matter, our paths had crossed again now later in life and as a consequence my wife was dead. What I hadn't yet married in my mind were the two men who seemed to inhabit the same body: The young intellectual artist who worked and studied hard to leave his home village and do well in the city; and the high achiever who could have been a lawyer or a high ranking diplomat. So why and when did he become a sadistic terrorist, an arms dealer and a drugs runner? Was it the death of his brother that drove him or his patriotic love of Greece? Is there a woman in the story that I can't see from the file? I sense that the ageing mother isn't the only matriarchal figure in this saga. I would track him to Greece and that would be the end of it.

I watched sunrise from the deck and thought about what supplies we needed to buy and started to study the tides and times for the next leg of our journey. I was excited about the prospect of sailing the Mediterranean instead of the Atlantic it was less daunting and brought me a step closer to my destiny which now seemed intertwined with Demetri's. Was I seeking revenge or just looking adventure? Did I really want to bring this killer to justice or find out more about what was motivating him? The sky was the colour of peach flesh and the sea a sort of bluey-green. Arthur came to find me carrying the lead in his mouth; it was time to go to the shops.

Armed with fresh loaves of bread and croissants still warm from the bakery, some cheeses, various salads and slices of chorizo, whole salamis, olives, I felt like a veritable delicatessen walking back to *Oystercatcher*. The Mediterranean was still green but the sky was changing from peach to that bright sunflower yellow you sometimes get before a storm. The breeze was rapidly stiffening to a gale and Arthur and I were quick to baton down the hatches and we ate our croissants and drank hot chocolate in the comfort of our little galley while hail stones the size of golf balls rained down all around us. With my sixth sense reawakened I left the dog cowering and went up to have a look at possible damage. I don't know what I was expecting to find but through the glimmering film of solid rain which hung between us and the shore I thought I saw a familiar silhouette and heard the whine of a motorbike engine beyond it. The yacht herself looked fine as I had in fact tied everything down the night before having checked the long-range forecast.

I went back inside and scoured today's newspapers for a whiff or a coded whiff of what our business might be all about. Something caught my eye in Gibraltar's English-speaking daily, a feature about a new breed of Greek billionaire who unlike previous generations were not content to rely on the assumed patronage of governments, institutions, families and were taking cultural and economic matters into their own hands by buying up land and businesses; not for the tourists but for themselves, the article was called Greece for Greeks. A group of young Athenian multi-millionaires had apparently formed a real estate company who now had properties as far afield as London, New York and Amsterdam and investment was also being made in shipping as per Greek tradition, hence the Gibraltar connection. With all its bunkering the tiny island handled something like ninety-three per cent of the world's cargo ships and anybody remotely involved would of course be making large amounts of money, all legitimately of course. Back home in Greece whole islands could be protected from foreign investment, simply by buying them. It went against an unwritten rule dating back centuries that the land could not be owned by an individual but it was not technically illegal.

Arthur made impromptu noises and farted in his sleep which meant I was more than willing to open the hatch again and much to my relief the storm clouds had passed. The granite edifice still towered above us but it was now gleaming white again and the sea beneath us was blue. All I had to do now was top-up fresh water tanks, clean out the bilge pumps, refresh chemical toilets and buy more fuel.

CHAPTER TWELVE

Jane was met by the police and the paramedics at the top of the boat slope. They put a foil blanket round her shoulders and offered her a cup of hot sweet tea before walking slowly towards the house and the ambulances. She saw Peggy being put into a body bag and lifted onto a stretcher. Jane was amazed at how delicate and dignified it all was, from complete strangers who doubtless did this sort of thing every day. She started crying and the female paramedic and the PC who escorted her looked solemn and squeezed her shoulders.

As they walked the length of the now floodlit garden there was another body bag and Jane wondered if Peggy had killed the guard? Outside, the house was full of police officers, some plain clothed, some in uniform and some armed who looked more like anti-terrorist specialists. Inside there were forensic detectives with their overalls and goggles on and a white gazebo had been set up against both the front and back doors. Jane took it all in subliminally as she was escorted to the back of a waiting ambulance.

'Hello love,' a kind man, one of the ambulance crew, said.

'They're going to take you to hospital as a precaution. Once they've checked you out we will want to ask you one or two questions, I'm afraid,' explained the female PC.

'Is Daddy OK?' Jane asked as she was directed to lie back and get strapped into her chair beneath a thick orange blanket.

'He's lost a lot of blood and we've taken him to hospital. More than that I can't tell you, I'm afraid. Try and rest.' The female officer nodded at the paramedic and once the driver had been given the signal the back doors were closed and they sped off to the infirmary with blue lights flashing.

Jane had her wounds dressed and X-rays were taken to see if any bones had been broken. She was given her own room and something to make her sleep while a drip in her arm steadily replaced sugars and salts lost during the incarceration period. The police were allowed five minutes of questioning while she was still awake but the nurse stayed in the room to make sure the interrogation didn't over run.

'I understand this might be difficult for you but we'd like to ask a couple of questions tonight, and then another officer will continue tomorrow if the doctors allow it, is that OK?'

'Yes, that's fine,' Jane nodded sleepily.

'Do you have any idea who these people were that did this to you, or why?'

'Absolutely no idea,' she shook her head.

'How many kidnappers were there?'

'Three that I saw but I think there were may have been two or three others, I don't know.'

'OK, thank you, we'll ask you to try and describe those men for us tomorrow. And how many people were being held captive with you?'

'It was just me and Peggy and Arthur, her dog. Then we discovered my dad was also a prisoner.'

'We saw a man leaving on a boat, was he one of the kidnappers?'

'No, he came to rescue us.'

'Was it someone you knew?'

'No.' The lie came instinctively; she felt she had to protect John.

'And did you know Peggy?'

'No.'

The nurse ended the question session and Jane fell fast asleep.

The next morning James still looked gaunt and pale but his stump had been properly looked at and he was as stable as could be expected before going into emergency plastic surgery later in the day. Jane sat next to the bed and didn't know where to start. He looked at her and raised a wan smile but it was as if something had changed between them.

'Are you OK, Daddy? How the hell did it happen?'

'Two of the goons were supposed to just scare me I think, but then they ended up removing my hand with a chainsaw.'

'Oh God…' Jane grabbed one of the grey recycled kidney-shaped sick bowls and threw up. 'Fuck, that's just horrid. But why you, how do you even know them?'

'Let's just say I borrowed some money from the wrong people.'

'That old chestnut,' Jane said under her breath and she sighed in disappointment. 'Jesus what kind of money problems have you got Daddy? You don't have a drink problem. Is it drugs, or gambling?'

'I'm your father Jane, you can't talk to me like that, baby.'

'I can bloody well talk to you how I like! We were nearly both killed for God's sake!'

'It was supposed to be easy money. All we had to do was tell them when the man visited and how often he went to his boat.' He wasn't looking at his daughter his eyes were fixed at an invisible point on the wall, 'Couldn't have been simpler really.'

'Which man are you talking about, and why couldn't you just make more money with the gallery or the properties?' As if she didn't already know which man. Jane was shocked, it was a seismic moment in a girl's life when her father fell from grace, putting into question everything she'd ever thought was true and real and making it impossible to trust him ever again.

'I'm so sorry Jane, I had no idea they were going to involve you, that they could hurt you.'

'Just tell me one thing. What do you know about the Greek-looking one?'

'Not much to be honest. He is Greek, from the mountains I think but now lives on one of the islands.'

'What's his name Daddy, which island is it?'

'The less you know about that man the better, I would have thought. Stay away from him, Jane.' His eyes refocussed and James winced in pain. He reached for the cream-coloured remote control and pressed the red button for the nurse to come and administer more pain killers. Jane kissed him on the forehead and left with tears in her eyes.

Jane had been to Greece before once or twice including sailing amongst some of the islands with friends but she realised she knew next to nothing about the country's history and the broader geography. She started to brush-up on everything she didn't know from the culture to the political history and the language. The internet was full of interesting stories, many she realised she already knew, but no photographs of you-know-who. Her Greek was still a ghost.

Jane booked a cheap flight to Athens and started to get ready for her trip, not that there was much to prepare she was simply following her heart and nothing and no one was going to stop her. She understood that John was sailing and that it would take him about two weeks to get there and that he was going to Greece, of that she was in no doubt. It was in Fate's hands now and with her in Athens she stood a much better chance of finding both John and the Greek than she did at home worrying whether or not her father's hand graft would take.

She headed straight for Piraeus, the central port, on a whim really but tactically it was the jumping off point for many of the islands and she had a prescient feeling that John would have to acknowledge the Greek sea-faring authorities at some point and that point would be here. All she had to do was enjoy being in Athens, soak up a bit of culture and continue her research. Her fourteen-night stay had been booked and paid for in advance online, with a voucher that had given her a massive discount and it would avoid awkward questions checking in at The Triton Hotel. She wouldn't have to explain why a single female traveller was going to patrol the docks for two weeks instead of sunning herself topless on one of many hundreds of beaches. Most guests only stayed for one or two nights before catching a ferry to the islands or going back to the airport. In the event her anxiety had been unnecessary and she was greeted politely as just another paying foreigner, given a room key and told what time breakfast was served and where. Perhaps she wasn't the first guest who sought anonymity and got it.

Jane in her early twenties, blonde, not married, no kids yet, travelling alone was at the apex of her desirability curve. She looked around the breakfast room and wondered who she would go for if she was still looking, and then she thought that actually she didn't owe anything to John and for all she knew he didn't even have feelings for her anyway so maybe she *should* have a fling while she waited? But she was half joking. She was half tempted. She added a knife-tip's worth of budget strawberry jam and popped another min croissant into her mouth. She noticed that her first cup of coffee was nearly empty and wanted another juice. All the guests had opted for one-table-per-person which meant that soon any new arrivals would have to share. Through the net curtains there was no view from their third-floor dining room so looking surreptitiously at each other was pretty much the only game in town. Jane wiped her mouth with her napkin and took another look at the mixed race French or Algerian-French man over by the window. Maybe she wanted him to be Algerian-French in terms of her fantasy. He was about her age with short dark curly hair, dark brown eyes and pock-marked skin. He was handsome in a brutish way, softened by long eye-lashes and he would have kept her up all night she thought, that is if he wasn't gay. She had found him already seated when she arrived at 07:00 a.m. He appeared not to notice her. Another man appeared at the top of the narrow square-spiral staircase, maybe thirty Jane thought and probably English or American. He took the obligatory minute or so to work out where everything was and what to do and then started to place things on his tray; making toast, pouring coffee, finding the milk and wondering why some people had hot items and others didn't. A very round-for-her-age chef in whites with a big grin and rosy-red cheeks came out of an invisible kitchen with another tray of sausages and bacon and answered that question. Jane's was now the nearest table to him and he asked politely if he may sit down and share it with her?

'Please, be my guest,' she said, and got up to get more coffee and juice.

When she came back he smiled and asked, 'So, what brings you to Athens? Or should I say to Piraeus?' Clearly not at all shy and therefore not British, she surmised. Already she liked him.

109

'I'm meeting a friend here. He's arriving by boat.' Jane returned the smile and sipped her new coffee.

'These little croissants are kind of cute aren't they?' He pronounced it crassONT and held the miniature pastry up to the light before popping it into his dentally perfectly mouth. Definitely American. 'Jay, I do apologise,' he stood up holding his napkin in one hand and offering the other to Jane. They shook hands and he sat down again, 'Here on business but thought I'd do a little island hopping in between conferences.'

Jane needed a cigarette and made her apologies, 'Nice to meet you Jay, I'm Jane. Excuse me I'm going to go outside and contribute to the air pollution.' She knew already that there was a smoking section outside on the balcony. They both laughed.

'Say, I'm thinking about getting the Metro train thing to the Parthenon this morning, see the Acropolis. Maybe you fancy it if you're free? Don't worry about money it's all tax deductible when you're with me.' Had he been English Jane would have been appalled and said "no" instantly, but the invitation framed so politely coming as it did from a rich foreigner she could hardly refuse.

'Reception in thirty minutes?' she smiled coyly.

Reception had both an artificial fish tank with fish set in stillness in aspic or plastic and an artificial beach complete with pebbles and starfish and seahorses set beneath Perspex that you had to walk over in order to get to the desk. Damien Hirst would have been proud. The pervading colour scheme was orange on gold and perhaps the biggest surprise of all was that the brightly coloured

110

wrapped sweets in a giant bowl were real and could in fact be eaten. Jane couldn't decide if it was wanna-be Hong Kong or just pure Piraeus? With Jay not down yet she went outside to stand on the kerb and smoke. To her left downhill towards the port was the end of the road where taxis, cars, mopeds, motorbikes all had to turn around in order to go back up to the main road or park and visit the fish market. The market was part of a pedestrianised mall consisting of restaurants and cafes and covering half a block. Twenty-first century Athens traded on the fact that it hadn't been trendy, or let's say affluent, since the 1980s but it was still proud. The Olympics money was also long gone and whole swathes of the city felt like a faded haircut photograph in a barbershop window. The appeal, Jane felt as she smoked was that they didn't care and just carried on. Deep reserves of resilience and also faith in their own way, it didn't matter what they were told to do or not to do, they had their way and that was laid down by the Ancient Greeks long ago and this way was not ever going to change. So the motorbikes raced and the taxis sped along and the mopeds weaved in and out of incessant traffic and the ferries docked and the container ships stranded by debt laid themselves to rest in the middle of the sea and the rich kept themselves to themselves and the poor were ignored and the tourists came and kept the economy afloat. She found herself wandering downhill to where the stray cats were eagerly watching the fish market opening up. As the plastic containers were emptied and the dregs thrown into the gutter the cats lapped up the bloody fish ice.

Jay emerged from the hotel lobby briefly frantic that he couldn't see her but then ebullient as he spotted her, 'Jane,' he screamed with both arms open wide, 'Let's go baby!' He was dressed as only Americans abroad can be in a sort of urban explorer's outfit that covered all possible

111

eventualities; discovering a lost tomb, having lunch with a beautiful lady, not being robbed in a busy thoroughfare while still being thin enough to feel cool in a hot place. And if all else failed and a change of clothes at the hotel later on wasn't possible it could also be worn to dinner. He had more pockets than a snooker table.

Jane burst into giggles and rather than say anything emasculating she simply patted him on the shoulder and said, 'Yes Jay, let's go.'

As they talked animatedly and walked in the direction of the Metro, unbeknownst to them the hotel door opened again and another man stepped out, an Algerian-French man. He put on his Aviators and looked both ways before crossing the street to head in the same direction.

CHAPTER THIRTEEN

Demetri was ready to implement his end game and deploy the virus. He had indeed fled The Pines at the sound of the approaching police and despite the apparent confusion he not only had what he wanted but had also succeeded in flushing out his nemesis, Mike. He couldn't see him but felt his invisible hand pulling the strings and had no doubt that with John's help, as he had foreseen, the puppet master would have to show himself before the end. There was no time to grieve over the foot soldiers he had lost.

Demetri flew straight to Karpathos and as he always did immediately on landing removed his suit and tie and shoes and walked out of the airport in shorts and a vest. He loved this island as much as he loved the woman who'd introduced him to it in the 1970s, Katerina. She brought him on the ferry from Athens, his first time on a big ship and he marvelled at their entrance into Pigadia in between the bare dark green limestone mountains. At university away from his mother's tight-rein and in the midst of a worldwide sexual revolution there was fun to be had for a barefoot shepherd from the mountains. Suddenly there were girls everywhere but Katerina was different and he knew that straight away. Losing her was worse than the death of his brother and the weight of the combined grief was enough motivation for him to prove to the gods they'd taken these two souls too soon.

The second largest of the Dodecanese islands, Karpathos was only ceded back to Greece from Italy in 1947. It was its own secret little kingdom and the village

113

Katarina took him to high up in the mountains an even greater secret.

Olympos. They'd walked most of the way but then she allowed them to take a lift from a relative who'd picked them up in his jalopy not climbing any faster than they were really on such a steep road, but it was romantic and fun to sit on the tailgate and watch as the island beneath them disappeared at an alarming rate and the harsh sunlight glare changed to velvety shade the colour of feathers. To share the tailgate with each other and eat pomegranates and almonds and sit in silence was a magic he hadn't known in his one man battle against the world. The kitbag that he threw into the back of the tiny three-wheeled tow-truck contained a gun and ammunition but he didn't dare say anything about his partisan activities; that could wait. The opalescent village appeared like a mirage nestled in a giant's bosom giant and Katerina's house, a simple white and blue cottage hewn from the rock above a precipice that fell away to the sea thousands of feet below was like nothing he'd seen at home in the central highlands and his eyes as well as his heart were opened for ever more.

Demetri walked from the airport to his latest church-building project which was about halfway between Pigadia and Olympos. Perched high above the sea on cliffs more frequented by goats then people the chapel site was in the corner of two stony fields each with a dozen olive and a half-dozen lemon trees. His only company was donkeys who brayed occasionally showing off their alarming teeth and equally alarming appendages, and a village guard dog who had taken to following him there whenever he was at work. On certain days Demetri would ring the bell of this St. Thikon's church all on its own and on certain other days in conjunction with the island's other churches, many of which had also been built by him. The monks had nurtured Demetri's artistic streak from childhood especially when it became apparent that his brother was going to follow a criminal path. They taught him how to repair and paint the religious icons adorning them with gold leaf, and touching them up with deep reds and dark browns and blacks. With his bare feet and bare hands he also learned to construct and repair the little whitewashed chapels that housed them. These were skills he never forgot but they stayed latent as he became a young man and spread his wings.

This chapel was almost complete and the old ladies tasked with looking after it had already put in the sand-filled candle holder, a twelve-pack of bottled water, their cleaning products and a small bottle of resinated wine. He was just adding the finishing touches to the final icon and this would be the last night he spent here.

Demetri had tried returning to the mountains over the years and several times he had been shielded from the authorities by the same monks, but his increasingly elderly parents were proud of the fact that he'd gone off to make it in the West and he owed it to them to disappear somewhere else to maintain the illusion. Karpathos had been chosen for him by the only woman he had ever loved, and there he would stay, even without her. He gazed up at the stars from the blanket beneath the almond trees and thought of his one big secret. It had burned inside him now for so long that he wondered how he would ever let it be known by other people. His nostrils were filled with the scent of the sweet earth that he lay on and the nut and fruit oils of the trees above him. He would sleep now knowing that part of his soul had been forever rendered in whitewash, paint and cement inside this holy chapel of St. Thikon but the fire that burned in him would not be extinguished by one simple act of penitence and faith. There were other churches to build and other gifts to lay at their feet.

Fishing from a boat didn't come as second nature to a mountain boy but Demetri had learned over the years how to do it and how to sail and sew his nets and set out late and return early with the village fishing fleet, spending all night sometimes miles into the open ocean. He could also swim out from the shore with a spear and come back with octopus. And it was these and other sojourns amongst the nearby uninhabited islands which had led to his discovery, the discovery that would be his chance to finally put his name on the lips of all the Greek people and make him a hero. If these words travelled as far as his home village before the death of his mother, then he would have done his work well. He imagined the newspaper headlines being read out-loud to her by one of the other yia-yias as they shared the good news and ate halva and sweet preserved fruits and drank coffee, all inside the house away from the prying eyes of the men. And in the cafés too his father would hear of it and they would drink ouzo and raki with their morning backgammon, shaking their heads and saying 'Bravo!'

It was a tomb, a high-status burial chamber filled with artefacts and it appeared intact. Nobody had seen what he saw for three thousand years. His little island was hilly like most of his beloved Greek Republic and maybe two square kilometres in size. Uninhabited and not farmed in living memory it simply sat proudly under the sun nestled between Karpathos and Rhodes. There were visible ruins which suggested that goatherds had at one time built

116

stone walls and shelters and the caves had perhaps been lived in much further back in prehistory but there were no houses or boat jetties. Nothing to excite rich Greeks or wealthy expats. Demetri would arrive by boat and moor up in an inlet on the far side of the island invisible to everybody including passing boats and ferries. The octopus and squid fishing was good here but what drew him initially was the prospect of building a chapel on the hill's highest point to honour Katerina. He had come here many times with her and they'd dreamed of building a house together and raising a family, if only they were rich enough to buy it.

After her death the Olympos priests and elders had given him permission to build a shrine in her honour on the highest peak. For ten years he had worked alone, carrying all the necessary materials up from his private bay to the top of the island on his back, including the water containers needed for mixing cement, all without any help. It was during his search for a fresh water source on the mountain that he had uncovered the tomb. It was well hidden and perhaps only a true stonemason like him would have been able to detect the sheen of hand-hewn stone through the thickness of undergrowth that covered it. Lain hidden for so long he had no reason to suspect that people would come here but then on that auspicious day he suddenly saw a large white cabin-cruiser at the tip of the island.

To his dismay they anchored, swam ashore and started to climb up over the rocks. Demetri walked carefully down through the steep wooded slopes to a point where he could hear and see them but not be noticed. They were Greeks, young and wealthy and from the snippets of conversation he heard were here to buy the

117

island. He traversed the ridge to a point along the beach that wouldn't startle them too much and casually appeared as if he'd just been swimming.

He greeted them in formal Greek, introduced himself and asked, 'How may I help you?'

'Who are you if you don't mind us asking?' said one of the young men, there were four of them two men and two women wearing swimming trunks and bikinis respectively. Demetri was overdressed in his shorts and a tee-shirt.

'I'm an architect. I'm constructing a chapel on top of the hill.' He pointed upwards just to emphasise his legitimacy. 'I might ask you the same question, this is a private island.'

The same young man, their nominated leader stepped forward, 'We represent a group of Greek property investors called Andrianakis Consortium and we're interested in purchasing this island. Our research reveals that it belongs to one Pegasus Holdings Ltd. Would that be you by any chance?'

'It isn't, but I know them. Would you like me to pass a message?'

'Well, they've had it since 1974 and might be open to an offer, seeing as they haven't really developed it at all.'

'Where can they reach you?' Demetri's body language was all pent-up rage but he checked himself and adopted a more relaxed pose.

'We'll give you a card, hang on.' The three others dove into the sea obediently and swam back out to the boat. The two other men, one old and one young remained awkwardly on the island, neither breaking the silence until the third man returned with a laminated business card.

'I hope it's still readable,' he said and it was.

As the cruiser sped away, its occupants not waving, Demetri's mind was already hatching a plan. He was a pragmatist and problems were there to be solved. In his other life he was well aware of the Andrianakis Consortium and their activities. He'd never heard of Pegasus Holdings but it could only be the Americans or British and 1974 meant the end of the Colonels' military regime, one year after the student protest and its bloody aftermath.

That night with the chapel built in Katerina's honour nearly completed, he had gone back to the main island and not up to the mountains and Olympos but from Pigadia over to Piraeus on the ferry and from there to Athens in a fast car with tinted windows moving north to a villa where he gained access with a password not heard there since the 1970s which itself set in motion a chain of events that could not be undone. The older man, an American Greek and ex-Ambassador waited by the glass-bottomed infinity pool for his guest to be brought through. He lit a cigar and poured himself a drink. The house was dated but back on-trend, all black polished marble and square-cut glass. In place of statues were orb-like water features and one or two ornamental palms set in amphorae filled with gravel. The artwork was all inside but big and minimalist, worth hundreds of thousands in the 1980s and millions now, giant canvasses with tortured

119

swirls of acrylic paint and scrolls of gold leaf. But it was the view that kept him there, that and the history, his personal history as well as mankind's history, the view straight across to the Parthenon. Demetri may have been there in '73 but he was there in '44 when the British tanks came. A secret history he knew all about. This day, his last, had been a long time coming.

'Sir,' started one of the staff.

'It's OK I know, thank you. Come in Demetri, please have a seat. May I offer you a drink?' The nonagenarian struggled to get up from his recliner and gave up.

'Good evening, Dan. No, thank you.' There was a pause while the older man smoked. 'I've come to ask you a question.' Demetri said, still pacing, oblivious to the splendour of his surroundings. As a Greek he felt this view was his for eternity anyway.

'Go ahead, what's troubling you my friend. It's been a long time.' The things we did as younger men, Dan thought to himself. As young men with absolutely no fear for our lives and no fear of the consequences. "If only I'd known then what I know now." He topped up his glass with brandy and took a little pull on the cigar. It was a good smoke, a Cuban Cohiba Corona Especial. 'You don't smoke? These are rather good.' He genuinely wanted his guest to share what he was enjoying.

Demetri sat down opposite the old man but leaned in towards him a little bit too close for comfort. 'There's a small uninhabited rock next to Karpathos, we locals call To Nisí. I'm building a chapel there in honour of

God, The Virgin Mary and a very special lady from Olympos who passed away. It is a holy island. Today I was visited there by young Greeks calling themselves the Andrianakis Consortium who want to buy it. They say that the title deeds are in the name of Pegasus Holdings Ltd. and have been since 1974. Is it possible that the password I used to get in to see you tonight and the name of this mysterious shelf company are not connected?' He paused for breath and stood up again. 'Please tell me what I don't want to know, Dan.'

'Please remember that we were all a lot younger then, yourself included Demetri. If I tell you, you have to promise me you won't start a war.'

'I want to end a war not start one.' His shoulders relaxed and he sat back down. 'You said something about brandy and cigars?'

Dan signalled for his aide to come and administer to Demetri while he, the elder statesman puffed on his cigar again and savoured the smoke. It was a warm night, a beautiful night and this high up it was easy to forget the traffic sounds from below. In fact it was easy to forget the metropolis entirely. He chose his words carefully, 'After 1973, a young man came forward with homemade movie footage from the protest. It was never made public knowledge and we never released its contents but it gave us great leverage in political circles.' Neither man spoke, Demetri was just listening. Dan continued, 'Your island, To Nisí, was payment for the film.' He'd already said too much and there was no going back from here.

'A student then, a comrade? Like you say we were all a lot younger in 1973.' Demetri lay back on his ottoman and tried to play back those events in his mind. Then it dawned on him that the young man he was searching for was also on Dan's payroll. The Americans had hedged their bets well.

'I bet he was British,' Demetri said but didn't expect an answer and now the pieces of the mosaic were starting to fall into place. He stood up to leave. 'Thank you, Ambassador, you have been most gracious.'

This time Dan did manage to come to his feet, 'You're very welcome old friend, and good luck.'

On his way past the aide-de-camp Demetri whispered to him, 'Come with me if you want to live,' but he had decided to stay. Less than a minute later while Demetri sat in the back of the limousine two men in balaclavas and black commando outfits came up the stairs Demetri had just vacated. Automatic pistols with silencers attached were the order of the day and both men, the ex-Ambassador and his aide, were shot neatly through the forehead. It was never meant to resemble a robbery just assassination, a vendetta pure and simple.

It was over twenty years since Demetri had visited his cousin in England and played cricket against some of her colleagues in the Cambridge University parks. She had told him what she could about her work in London in the laboratory. The work itself was extremely interesting and he'd gleaned from what she couldn't say that they were dealing with deadly biological weapons. She'd also mentioned that she had something in common with two of the men in the lab who had both worked in Greece in the 1970s. Yes Demetri remembered Cambridge in the 1980s very well now, and that picnic in particular, punting with

122

Panayota and her telling him all about her colleagues. The cricket he also remembered, the monks had taught him spin bowling and that was his forte so he had been brought into bat as a nightwatchman and just as he was about to open up his shoulders the next morning and start hitting a few, one of the Englishmen had got him out first ball.

CHAPTER FOURTEEN

The Department wasn't normally in the habit of keeping an eye on its retirees, it simply wasn't cricket. Being left alone was considered one of the privileges. If however one of the said retirees was brought to the Department's attention that was an entirely different matter and could be dealt with a little differently. The afternoon that shots were fired in a Gloucestershire field, Mike had been on the golf course in Godalming Surrey. The following day when it was reported that people had been killed in a marina not far from Weston-Super-Mare, he had been having Sunday lunch at a Michelin-starred pub near Bray. Officially, of course, Mike didn't know where John had gone since changing his identity but unofficially he had a rough idea where their bungalow was and these reports had become interesting enough for him to skip dessert and take coffee back at the office. He made his excuses to the junior minister and his charming press secretary with whom he had been skirting round the pressing matter of re-armaments and called his wife from the car to say he wouldn't be back for supper, sorry. She, of course, was used to such phone calls since his promotion and merely switched the oven off, changing her mind about what she was, or rather wasn't, going to cook. Mike had sat with the surveillance operators, two of which were always on duty even on a Sunday, and he had even feigned disinterest when the cameras appeared to show known associates of a certain Greek individual who had long been of interest to INTERPOL but hadn't officially done anything wrong in public since the 1970s.

'Surveillance, sir?' One of the listeners had asked automatically.

'Oh yes definitely but let's go level three for now. Ask the helicopters from RAF Benson and the Air Sea Rescue boys to take snapshots for us.'

'No drone, sir?'

'They'd spot a drone a mile away.'

Mike carried the weight of his office lightly but inside the thin frame was a heavy brain whose synapses were all firing off shots to one another as he tried to piece together the fragmented jigsaw of his early life in the Department and equate it to the decisions he was about to make now. Syntagma Square 1973 had looked like any other Athenian demonstration, long-haired students in the square (he still had hair then) plus a procession of two or three hundred believers all carrying placards and banners held high. They walked slowly behind one solitary pick-up with a vocal Demetri standing up at the back and shouting for all he was worth through the megaphone, laying out his agenda for change. Demetri spoke not only for the downtrodden Greek students but for the Greek people and the proletariat worldwide, it was the global call of socialism, justice and equality for all. They would not stop marching, he said, until all those wrongly imprisoned were freed, until all students went to higher education for free, until all politicians declared their sources of income, until all journalists were protected from assassination, until all the rich were brought to task and made to redistribute their lands amongst the people. How can any man be free if the elected few still monopolise the wealth of the many? He called for equal rights for women and all people regardless of race. Against the backdrop of just another strike for the University everyone had taken the day off and taken to the streets. Three hundred became five hundred became a thousand. In Athens it wasn't unusual to make yourself heard this way, coffees were carried in plastic cups and cigarettes were lit. Except that this one had gone the distance, had gone horribly wrong in fact. Shots were fired teargas filled the streets and the hot orange glow of street lights mingled with cars and shopfronts up in flames, police horses reared and eyes ran red with blood and the effects of the gas. For several frantic minutes nobody knew what had gone wrong and was that a tank through the manmade mist?

Athens was Mike's first posting after Northern Ireland. And frankly he was glad to be out of Ireland. Always the quiet one Mike made up for what he lacked in looks and social skills by being observant, he was also a good scientist but his real skill he'd discovered was being able to sniff out opportunities. The girls had *implored* Mike to join them on the march, he was so deliberately nondescript that they all loved his company, almost as if he was a token girlfriend, they just felt sorry for him, but he would have gone anyway to hear what Demetri was going to say. In fact he was being paid to record it. But Mike had gone one step further and filmed it, and it was this footage that would cement his promotion path as well as his pension fund for the future. Few people have the presence of mind to step outside of a moment they're already in and look at it objectively but those that manage it invariably walk away richer, or psychologically damaged, or both.

From the outside it wasn't clear how it all flared up and turned from peaceful protest to fully-fledged riot with retaliation. Shots were fired as well as teargas and screams rose up through the smoke, students fleeing came up against riot shield barriers and horses' hooves in the dark and confusion. Mike kept filming ignoring friends who pulled on his coat tails for him to leave. He watched as Demetri ducked below the cab momentarily and reappeared clutching a rifle instead of a megaphone, his face obscured now by a bandana pulled up over his mouth and nose. Using the cab as a platform he fired shots through the smoke in the direction of the police and the tank. His muzzle flashes and even the sound of the shots swallowed up by the noise. He jumped down to the ground and said something to the driver who started to inch the vehicle forward towards the police front line. Mike followed Demetri into the melee and now there were gaps in the smoke and as the truck rolled past it revealed Demetri kneeling with his rifle raised and aimed directly at the Chief of Police who stood up in a Jeep and gesticulated at his troops. One shot to the throat and he tumbled to the ground, enveloped in mist, Demetri jumped into the back of the pick-up and banged on the cab. They disappeared into the night and Mike was also gone into the diaspora.

Retaliations against the students were harsh and summarily organised, student halls locked down and all individuals who'd ever voiced anti-establishment thoughts were arrested as dissidents and terrorists and sent to the cells in the back of riot police vans. Mike had the luxury of slipping through that particular cordon to wait it out in the British Embassy and not in his digs. Anxious friends who searched for him in vain assumed the worst that he had also been captured or even killed. Reports said that two dozen protesters had been killed in the square by snipers while three police were injured and one killed. It was a long sleepless night for Mike but by morning (when they hadn't come for him) he had regained control of his emotions and the situation. Once it was known what he had in his possession it wasn't the British who came forward but the Americans who emerged as the highest bidders and made him an offer he couldn't refuse. It was all done in a terribly civilised way but in return for Mike handing over the film and any copies, "There weren't any copies were there?" he would be given a Greek island. In a shelf-company name obviously, and uninhabited, but it would be his in-perpetuity and inarguably beautiful. Who knows you might even find gold or oil there! Do the Greeks know you've got it? No, good, the fewer people who know about this the better. Let's keep the channels open old boy, that's what you say isn't it? And maybe we can help each other again. The exchange was made, the papers were drawn up and signed and Mike had his own island. More a lump of rock really, out in the Carpathian Sea next to Karpathos.

Mike's next cover posting was as an English teacher on Crete. He absolutely loved it and spent the best part of ten years there and would have stayed longer if Dorothy hadn't been so determined to give birth in an English hospital in England. Frequent visits to Athens and London kept him up-to-date with what was happening at the then Foreign Office and made him feel important despite his junior rank. Surreptitiously he still had contact with the Americans, usually on Rhodes, and during these visits he would sometimes permit himself a boat trip out to The Rock as he called it, his own private Gibraltar, and spend a day or two pottering about and grilling fish on the beach. The Americans were always quick to remind him how grateful they were that he had kept their arrangement secret and what a great job he'd done filming the events of 1973 for them. He was quick to point out that he had filmed for himself, but that seemed a little academic now.

The leader of the student protest, the one with the megaphone and the rifle, was becoming a person of interest and Mike was reminded that any information about him and/or his cell would never go amiss, and would always be rewarded.

And that's how Mike the double agent with a special interest in Pegasus was born. No one saw Mike as anything other than a small man who was quite good at his job and would probably get promoted soon. He didn't engender envy or generate suspicion he just went quietly about his business. He married Dorothy as soon as they knew she was pregnant, and they had a marvellous Greek wedding complete with smashing plates and dancing in the surf with his trouser legs rolled up and her wedding dress hitched above the knee. After the Colonels' regime fell and Greece began to get back on its feet economically with a tourism boom it was OK to be British again but his new cover didn't call for such an outspoken left-wing ideology, his tastes might be revolutionary in music, art, and books but once he boarded the boat to Rhodes or the plane to London it was all Queen and country and Dorothy couldn't have been more proud if they really were the Ambassador and his wife after all – a charade that she still played out to this day.

Pegasus himself surfaced in 1980s Europe under the guise of a lawyer with specialist interests in maritime law and fishing rights. He and Mike had met at a conference in Berlin and at another in Helsinki, although this one was under the umbrella of offshore gas versus nuclear reactors. The men didn't speak to each other, neither man representing his actual government, but Mike was building quite a dossier and tracing the financial transfers of Pegasus' business dealings could only mean that he was laundering money for a large criminal organisation or else creating a diverse investment portfolio for a very wealthy anonymous client. He could never prove links to the criminal underground or terrorism, and started to think that Pegasus might be legitimate – that his dealings all had to do with his passionate belief in freedom for his people and the Hellenic Republic. As he grew older Mike was reminded that he too had fought on those streets. And then it all stopped, Pegasus disappeared, the well ran dry and Mike and Dorothy were moved back to Dorking. There were Middle East postings (Oman, Dubai) but his career became all about London and the lab. He stuck at it long enough and played the politics so well that he rose through the ranks and avoided mandatory retirement. But there was a problem; whilst it was true that Mike was quiet and unassuming he was also fiercely ambitious and now that he'd had a taste of the good life he wasn't going to stop. Once home he made several investments, in the early to mid-1980s before anybody had to worry about money, buying up small estates in Derbyshire and Gloucestershire but then suddenly the American Pegasus money stopped coming in. He had to find a way of plugging the hole, to find a new bed-fellow, and he started to sleep around so-to-speak. Dorothy knew nothing of his portfolio and rising debts just as she knew nothing of his life as a double agent.

In all the years Mike and John worked together Mike was certain John didn't know about him being a double agent. The four of them Mike, Dorothy, John and Peggy had often holidayed and socialised together and had even been posted abroad in the same country but Mike would always let John have the mysterious mien about him of "maybe he works for the secret service." And John would not have known about his interest in Pegasus either.

The status quo had been exactly that for the duration of an entire generation when suddenly Demetri reappeared from nowhere and interrupted Mike's swing.

CHAPTER FIFTEEN

Jane subconsciously heard the high-pitched whine of a
motorbike engine climbing uphill and thought it was odd
given that they were on a pedestrianised path. It must be
on a separate road nearby she thought as they negotiated
another set of steps.

Meanwhile the Algerian-French man had also seen
the scrambler ignoring requests for it to stop and he broke
out into a run, pounding the marble steps beneath him in
its wake his lungs and legs burning, no match for the 500cc
engine and knobbly tyres.

As the noise grew louder in her ears Jane turned
round but the bike was on them and had already stopped.
The pillion passenger, helmeted and leather-clad jumped
off and grabbed Jane's handbag while the bike turned
round and revved its engine waiting for his accomplice and
scaring the already terrified crowd. Jay flung himself
unthinkingly at the rider on top of the yellow bike and
brought them both to the ground. Jay was a big man after
all. Through the crowd Jane recognised the face of the
Algerian-French man from the hotel who jumped in and
wrestled with the accomplice who had now drawn a gun
and was trying to shoot Jane. The Frenchman brought
down the bag-snatcher knocking the pistol out of his hand
and a shot was fired harmlessly into the air, then with his
body shielding Jane moved across to take on the bike rider.
But he was too late to save Jay; the motorcyclist was also
armed and had shot the American after their scuffle before
pointing the bike downhill to make his escape. The
Algerian-Frenchman squatted on his haunches to lessen

the downhill angle and fired two shots in quick succession, one into the bike and one into the back of the rider. Sirens sounded all around as Greek police started to arrive and the Parthenon security were quickly all over the scene. They arrested the pillion passenger and the biker, clearly injured, drove lamely through the fence and let the bike fall onto the street below. He threw down his helmet to help him run and nearly got killed crossing the busy road. There was a lot of shouting 'Eh, Malakas!' and the traffic had to screech to a halt again as the Algerian-French man in leather jacket and trainers flew past hot on his heels.

Jane lay on the foot slopes of the Parthenon with Jay's head in her lap, stroking his hair and telling him that everything was going to be fine. By now there was an armed police cordon around them. The green-clad paramedics arrived quickly and cut away Jay's multi-pocketed waistcoat and breathable safari shirt to patch and dress the gunshot wound but he was losing a lot of blood. They spoke Greek into their radios and presently another noise louder than the bike filled the air as a medevac helicopter appeared from nowhere did a quick surveillance sweep of the landing zone and came down right next to them as directed by the female crew while her male colleague stayed with Jane and Jay and held the drip aloft. Two more paramedics jumped out of the chopper and approached Jane, asking in English, 'Are you family, Ma'am?'

'No' she replied, 'just a friend.'

'We can only take him I'm afraid. You can come to the hospital in the ambulance.' He smiled and indicated the ground crew.

Meanwhile the other paramedic was talking to Jay, 'Hello sir, can you hear me? We're going to help you and take you to hospital in the helicopter, OK?' Jay seemed to nod from somewhere deep inside but his eyelids were firmly closed. They rolled him onto a lightweight stretcher already laid out on the ground behind him and with one deft lift he was up and into the helicopter. Jane could only watch and weep as the engine flared and the rotors quickened again taking them up above the rooftops and out of sight. She felt she was on the wrong end of a prison-break, the one left behind in the astonished exercise yard after the rescue.

Disconsolate and shocked with feelings of mistrust resurfacing, feelings which she'd managed to keep a lid on with the excitement surrounding her feelings for John, the paramedics and police escorted Jane to the hospital in the ambulance. There were tests and questions which she answered and she enquired about Jay but representatives of his company's lawyers had advised him not to speak to her, or at least that's what she was told. She understood intuitively that that wasn't the same as him saying he didn't want to speak to her. The hospital was hot and loud and far busier than she remembered a hospital in England ever being but it passed her by in a blur. With her tests passed and her hotel address taken, she was free to go and suddenly found herself smoking outside on the kerb. She wanted to walk for a bit and although she didn't really care where she was she got her bearings from the position of the Acropolis above her and made her way downhill towards civilisation, shops and bars. She passed a large white church with terracotta tiles on the roof and gold painted minarets. It was set back in a square framed by palm trees and the Orthodox chanting was being broadcast onto the street through a loud speaker. Jane crossed the

134

square where she found a large stray dog which followed her and wanted to sniff between her legs, she shooed it away and two lovers laying a bit too close to each other next to one of the benches. Her presence didn't deter them from what they had already started. She climbed the steps to the church and even before she entered through the glass-panelled door the shade of the porch was cooling and soothing. She gently pushed the door open and instantly smelled candle wax and incense and forgot about the world outside as she sat and stared up at the bright red icons dripping in gold. A larger-than-life Jesus seemed to look her right in the eye. Jane found some euro coins in her purse and lit three candles. She closed her eyes to make a wish and then went back to one of the pine pews where she knelt in prayer as the priest continued his nasal genuflecting aided and abetted by one old Greek lady and one young, slightly overweight, Greek boy.

After five minutes she left and went back out into the heat, this time looking for a metro stop and the train back to Piraeus and home to the hotel.

There was a knock on her door, scared she tentatively opened it and found the Algerian-French man standing there.

'Have lunch with me?' he suggested.

'You must be fucking joking!' Jane slammed the door in his face, but he continued to gently wrap his knuckles on it until she opened up again. This time just a little bit and she kept the chain on.

'Please, I'm a friend. You can't stay here anymore. Pack your bags and come with me. But first I'd like to take

135

you to lunch.' His exotic accent would have been romantic in any other setting but right now it just reminded her of being kidnapped and beaten up and she refused point blank to trust another man, especially a stranger, again.

'If I'd wanted to harm you I would not have saved your life. Here,' he said and pushed something across the floor through the gap, 'my ID. I'll be outside in the red Peugeot. Bring your things.' And then he added, 'and my ID.'

Jane glanced at the ID and turned it over in her hands, a European police identity card, INTERPOL maybe. It seemed real enough but who was paying his wages? Her heart said stay at the hotel and take her chances, but her head was telling her to at least get his side of the story and then work out what to do. As she went through her options she threw what few possessions she'd brought with her into her bag, emptied the bathroom of cosmetics into her makeup bag, checked under the bed and waited by the antiquarian lift. Nothing happened for twenty seconds and she remembered the ID was still on the bedside table, she went back for it and then ran down the stairs. The Triton reminded her of the wonky pyramids built by Edifis in *Asterix and Cleopatra* and she ran as fast as the architecture would allow. At the desk Jane went to check out but before she could open her mouth both the lady and the man on duty shook their heads smiling and said, 'Oxi, endaxi! Efcharisto.' And, 'Kalo taxidi, see you next time!' With some relief, Jane thought. Perhaps Giovanni had paid, she knew his name now.

The red Peugeot was directly opposite and Giovanni was smoking, talking on the phone and drinking coffee from a plastic cup all at once. He looked cool in his shades and still managed to get out, put her bags in the back and open the passenger door for her to get in. He didn't stop the phone call and didn't say anything directly to her. Jane didn't notice him start the car but all of a sudden they were driving uphill and into the traffic. The day was hot now and the sun shone hard on the windscreen in spite of its ten-inch shaded strip in blue and she opened the window and pulled her visor down.

'No, no, sorry. Put the window up!' Giovanni indicated frantically in sign language which also said sorry and switched the AC on full. In no time at all there was cool air circulating which smelled of hot car seats, cigarettes and secret agents who hadn't showered or slept for days. She was only briefly aware of which direction they were headed in but she thought it was away from Piraeus in roughly the direction of the airport. They joined faster traffic now and wove in and out of lanes a few times but always it seemed the sea was on their right and it quickly started to look less built up and became industrial rather than residential. Jane started to wonder where exactly he was taking her for lunch but didn't say anything out loud. At a turn-off Jane hadn't even seen they slowed down and left the highway and pulled up at what looked like a private ferry terminal. It was deserted and would be a good place to dispose of somebody Jane thought, maybe she could kill Giovanni and steal the Peugeot, put her photo on his detective badge, but she was joking and acknowledged that fatigue and hunger were making her cranky.

'Please,' Giovanni held open a smoked glass door and held out his other arm indicating that she should enter.

'Welcome, welcome,' the Maitre-D bustled in English, 'a nice table by the sea?' he put menus on the table in front of them and pulled out Jane's chair before pushing it back in with her on it and delicately draping the napkin in her lap. He spoke Greek with Giovanni and came back in seconds it seemed with bread, a big Greek salad, tzatziki, a litre bottle of water and a half-carafe of white wine.

He thanked the waiter and then said to Jane, 'I apologise for the wine,' Giovanni removed his shades and poured out two glasses, 'I mean maybe you would prefer a soft drink?'

Jane shook her head, 'This is fine, thank you.' But she was in no mood to be charmed, and she lit a cigarette and sipped the wine. The food could wait. The sea was flat like a mill pond and she watched the deep blue ripples lapping at the beach and had a flashback to Peggy being killed, to Daddy's hand being chopped off, to her being smashed in the face by a ringed fist and Jay being shot. She watched the rocks below the surface of the sea and brightly coloured fish swimming in and out of the pools of light.

'Are you OK? You should eat.' Giovanni was already eating. 'Should I order the main course? Is pork souvlaki OK or you'd prefer fish? Let's get both.' And he waved to the waiter.

'This is all very lovely,' Jane paused, 'But I still don't know who you are, or why you're protecting me and even who you're protecting me from! I'm not inclined to simply trust a stranger. Why should I trust a stranger?

Where are we even going? I should get back to the hotel and call the police.' She got up to leave.

'Wait, I am the police, please.' He stood up quickly and held her gently by the arm. 'He said to give you this,' Giovanni reached into his jacket pocket and gave Jane a small padded envelope. Inside it was a simple gold necklace with a St Christopher pendant. 'Your father just wants you to be safe, that's all.'

She hated the necklace and hadn't worn it since her parents' divorce, before her mother's death, and anybody could have got it from her childhood bedroom. She made up her mind then and there not to trust whichever side Giovanni was on and get out as soon as possible. To his face she said, 'You know Daddy, how is he?'

'Much better, they say he will be a good candidate for a prosthetic hand and will lead a relatively normal life again. It would have been easier to keep you safe if you'd stayed in England but I don't have orders to take you home, only to look after you as long as you choose to remain in Greece.'

Jane didn't believe a word. She smiled and ate, all the time thinking, 'Who the fuck are you, Giovanni? And where are you taking me?' Out loud she said, 'What is this place, some sort of private port?'

'Piraeus is good for tourists and big ships but there is another type of Greek who prefers to come and go a little more discreetly.' Right on queue a sleek looking cruiser came into view and dropped anchor a little way off the beach. A grey rigid inflatable was untied from the stern and a man got in and started its outboard motor, heading towards them to the shore.

The main courses arrived and Giovanni tucked in, pouring himself more wine. He indicated the new man and said, 'My colleague will take you to a safe house on one of the nearby islands. You will be safe there and when your friend arrives we will inform him of your whereabouts.'

Jane looked at the back and shoulders of the boat skipper staring out to sea and throwing pebbles. She couldn't be certain but the silhouetted outline looked familiar. She suddenly felt terrified and realised she had to make her escape sooner rather than later.

'I need to use the bathroom,' Jane said suddenly.

'Be my guest.'

'Is the boot open, I need my bag please,' She hoped she wouldn't have to explain why a lady might want to take her handbag to the ladies room.

'It's open.'

Jane took her bag and walked as nonchalantly as possible across the decking area, past the empty tables and back inside the restaurant. It was dark even with her shades off and looked like a 1980s night club more than a dining room but it didn't take long to locate the WC sign tucked away in the corner next to the main EXIT. She couldn't see anyone else either in the red neon-lit bar or through the kitchen's porthole windows. But to her dismay there was somebody in the ladies' room, a very smart young Greek woman who looked every inch a plain

140

clothed detective and had the confidence to go with it. She was filing her nails and apparently waiting for Jane.

'You can pee with the door open, then go back and enjoy your lunch.' Jane almost burst out laughing, they really wanted her to enjoy this lunch, wow! But she did need to pee and did as she was told. She came back to the mirror and put her handbag next to her on her left, with the female bodyguard to her right. Jane applied a little lipstick and made the appropriate puckering and un-puckering mouth motions. She put the lipstick back and picked up a small can of mace spray and quick as a flash gave her companion a face-full. The effects were instantaneous and the discomfort obvious. Jane took the opportunity to manhandle her into the same cubicle and grabbing her bag ran out through the front door and back into the glaring sunlight and hot dusty street. She ran without turning round as far as the main road and stopped in the shade of a tree to catch her breath and look for a bus stop. To cross the road here was suicide but she went quickly as soon as there was the slightest let up in the flow of traffic and made it to the other side. The nearest shelter was only fifty metres along the boulevard back towards town and she could also see the metro rails running parallel to the pedestrian path and the sea on the other side. She ran again still not caring about who was behind her and only stopped when she reached the bus shelter. She put her shades back on and wished she was carrying water like a proper tourist would be. No red Peugeot on the road and no sleek cruiser in the bay, hopefully they thought she was still in the loo. The bendy bus bore down on them looking as if it was going far too fast to stop but managed to pull up silently and the hydraulics let the front step down to kerb level. She got on and found a double seat to herself which was also near the back door just in

141

case. Jane lent against the hot glass and breathed a sigh of relief. If anybody was watching her they pretended not to notice but everybody seemed preoccupied with their phones.

It was still the middle of the day when the bus stopped in Piraeus and Jane got out. This area she knew a little bit and she ducked between the rundown tall buildings to visit a supermarket where she could buy food, water, fruit, plus hair dye and scissors. The brief interlude into an air-conditioned shop was welcome and actually did her quite a lot of good. She copied the Greek shoppers and munched pistachio nuts and grapes without buying them, as she walked round which were very delicious. From there she headed on foot straight to the cheaper part of town, past the burgeoning refugee camp by the police station and into the docks proper. The first budget hotel she came to called Pension Ariadne looked clean and cheerful enough and she found the proprietor on duty at the desk, clearly a businesswoman who didn't have time to siesta with the rest of Athens.

Ariadne, if that was her name, was a kind lady and Jane felt bad having to lie to her but she had to stay hidden, 'Yasas, good afternoon, do you speak English?' Jane smiled.

'Yes, I do. My son is having an English wife!! I love English!!'

'Perfect, I'd like a single en-suite room please for five maybe seven nights. I have money but I don't have my passport which was stolen at the airport. So I'm sort of stranded and waiting for friends who are sailing through

Greece and my new passport at the same time if that makes sense?'

Ariadne thought long and hard, there were strict rules about taking guests' details correctly Jane knew. 'Do you have a photocopy of your passport maybe, or perhaps you remember the number?'

'I don't, I'm so sorry.' And then Jane cried. The tears came more easily than she'd anticipated and she had to hold back the floods of emotion as they each realised their pent-up incubation period might be at an end.

Ariadne patted Jane's hands and said, 'There, there. You pay me OK? And we don't tell my husband. Endaxi?' She nodded solemnly avoiding eye contact, and the deal was done.

Jane also nodded, 'Of course, thank you so much. I'm sorry, signomi. I'm just very tired.'

'Cash or card?'

CHAPTER SIXTEEN

Once in her room Jane made sure the door was locked, turned on the aircon and the TV and planned to do her hair. She lay down on the bed to take off her shoes and woke up four hours later. She couldn't tell if it was day or night and didn't recognise the room she was in. It took two or three seconds of intense concentration to recall the events of the day and moving hotels and pretending she didn't have a passport. Jane should have dyed her hair before renting a room but she was new to this whole spying thing and figured she was allowed one or two rookie errors. Jane pulled opened the little glass windows and pushed open the folding shutters to reveal a little Juliet balcony and a spectacular view of the sea, crammed in between two derelict buildings and a gigantic crane. The sun was almost set and the sky was ultramarine turning black with scarlet and pink and yellow hues running through it towards the horizon.

Hungry, Jane opened her little fridge and started to make sandwiches from her supplies. Thank God she'd had the foresight to buy beer and she opened one to drink with her food before grabbing the plastic gloves and heading into the bathroom. She chose a music channel on the TV and listened as she showered and wet her hair. Jane couldn't remember the last time she was brunette; it must have been over ten years ago during a brief dalliance with all things Gothic after Mummy's passing. And the self-cut bob? She'd never done that it was just something she'd seen in the movies. It was quite tricky to arrange everything with so little shelf space and she settled for leaving the bottle of beer and its glass on the table by the TV in the bedroom which left just enough room on the glass shelf in front of the mirror for the hair dye and the scissors once she'd removed the complimentary soaps and tooth mug and put them on the toilet seat. With a towel wrapped round her waist and another towel on standby to brush any cut hairs from her body into the basin she made a blonde twist and pulled it in front over her right shoulder in order to start cutting the ends in the mirror. She repeated the manoeuvre over the left shoulder and soon had a semi-decent schoolgirl's bob. She laughed at the reflection of her fifteen-year-old self and wondered what she would have thought. Jane picked out all the hair from the basin and plug hole and put it in the plastic bag by the toilet. The dyeing process was simple enough and while she waited twenty minutes for it to work she sat watching the sky and drinking beer with her scalp fizzing and itchy. She wondered how far away John was?

Having eaten all her provisions and drank all the beer Jane was wide awake and not ready to try and sleep again so soon. She found herself meandering back towards reception and alone she lit a cigarette and studied the large map of Greece which was pinned to the wall above the low white Formica table.

'You are thinking about your friends?' Ariadne was on duty again, or still on duty, or always on duty. 'You know where they are?'

'I'm not sure,' Jane admitted.

'Sailing from England?' Ariadne was sharp as a knife beneath her hands-on-pinny hotelier guise, Jane could see that.

'Yes,' Jane said and put out her cigarette. Outside through the open door the port glowed orange under the street lights but if anything was louder than during the day as bars and nightclubs turned on their music. Mopeds whizzed up and down on the pavement outside. The air smelled hot and salty with a faint whiff of fish like a docks at rest.

Ariadne lifted the flap that allowed her to step out from behind the desk and she was clutching a tall half-litre bottle of beer and two small glasses, 'Me ya,' she said pretending to stroke her own hair and pointing at Jane's, then after some thought she said, 'It suits you.'

Jane was embarrassed, having almost forgotten she'd just gone from blonde to brunette in the space of sixty minutes.

Ariadne poured them a glass of beer each and chinked Jane's glass, 'Yamas!'

'Yamas!' Jane reciprocated.

'So,' Ariadne approached the map, and Jane could now see that the sailing routes were marked on it in different colours, 'from Gibraltar in summer, this one.' She smiled and maintained eye contact with Jane, suspecting that she might not be OK, and traced the southerly-most route of the two pictured, hitting Malta and passing south of Sicily before entering Greece at the southern Peloponnese or Crete.

It was suddenly dawning on Jane that John didn't have to register at Piraeus at all if his point of entry wasn't Athens, and clearly from the map it wouldn't be. She had a lot of thinking to do.

'Thank you Ariadne,' she said, 'Efcharisto poli.' They smiled at each other and started to drink the last of the beer. The hotel telephone rang and Ariadne was called back on duty leaving Jane to her thoughts. Jane lit another cigarette and idly flicked through the retro-tourism magazines which lay next to the ashtray. Jane wondered how they had never been thrown away, some of them were older than she was dating from the 1970s and 1980s but covered in thick see-through plastic they'd somehow survived and the timeless beauty of the Greek islands was, well, timeless. It reminded her that she still didn't know where her Greek adversary domiciled when he was at home. There were hundreds of islands. There it was in black and white, "of Greece's six thousand islands only 227 are inhabited." How in hell's name was she ever going to find John again and discover what was really going on?

After two days under Ariadne's watchful gaze Jane felt confident that nobody was going to find her new hotel or recognise her with brown hair, at least nobody who hadn't known her before. Trusting a lot to luck and instinct she decided it was time to do some research and start being proactive. Her plan was in two parts; one – to visit the library to look at archives on Greek organised crime, and two – to hang out where expat yachtsmen and women came in if they visited Athens. It was very tempting to mix with the locals and have breakfast in the docks near the hotel but her Greek wasn't good enough and in the end she didn't feel comfortable as a foreign woman. She settled for first coffee and cigarette of the day on the little wrought iron table outside Pension Ariadne and perhaps something a bit posher later, on her way back from the library. She wasn't going to glean any titbits in a language she couldn't understand. It had only been light for less than half an hour but Piraeus was already busy and

147

the traffic noise from the nearby streets loud and thrumming. The light was flat and harsh painting the sky an eggshell colour, the deeper Mediterranean blues not yet filtering through. Ariadne brought the hot coffee and a little basket of homemade sweet breads which were warm and delicious.

The National Library of Greece was in a place called Phaleron Bay and part of a futuristic Ark-like arts complex. It was busy but not overcrowded and Jane soon found a helpful librarian who helped her get set-up with a micro-fiche unit and instructions on how to search the archive. There was also a PC she could use for articles that had been put on disk. There were one or two tourists but very few foreigners using the research facilities. Jane soon hit upon the complicated political history of modern Greece and didn't want to get bogged down in WWII history but she followed the thread of left-wing insurgency and communism. The Student Massacre of 1973 caught her attention and she was shocked by some of the photographs – dead bodies and badly injured students – but drawn to the styles of the day, long hair, beards, flared jeans and tight tops with frilly cuffs. She could imagine the scene, and felt empathy for the students who were peacefully marching when the authorities shot at them.

The library aircon was on, and Jane was enjoying it, so she was surprised to smell body odour and carefully tried to sniff her own armpits to make sure it wasn't coming from her. It wasn't of course but Jane soon became aware of a presence nearby, a young man who was watching her. Dressed like a returning Vietnam Vet. complete with red bandana and combat jacket with CND patches on the shoulder, he was a sort of Greek Che Guevara meets John Lennon, wearing round gold-rimmed

148

spectacles. He was an amalgam of political ideologies and fashions. He wore high-top D.M.'s and green camouflage parachute trousers. No wonder he's sweating, thought Jane, the young man seemed more interested in what she was studying than he was in her which irked Jane a little bit, 'Can I help you?' she turned around and said in a clearly irritated tone.

Thinking he'd found a kindred political spirit this was the invitation he'd been waiting for, and he came over and offered his hand, smiling. The hand looked as sweaty as his spotty complexion and Jane declined politely, but he didn't seem too perturbed. His jacket had pin badges of the American flag, the Greek flag and a guitar, or was it a bouzouki?

'1973, The Polytechnic Massacre, such a pivotal event,' He shook his head in mourning for the fallen comrades. 'You don't' mind if I practice my English on you do you? It's been a while since I learned.' His teeth were almost all worn away and hard to look at; his mouth was just gummy and combined with the stubbly beard growing through the acne Jane was finding the conversation difficult.

'Did you look through the photographs?' He leaned over her and started to flick through the scenes of the demonstration. 'They say on the actual day that one of the students was filming but the footage was never released, it was obviously suppressed.'

'By whom?' Jane was a little bit interested despite herself.

'You tell me, by the Greeks, by the USA, by the British.' The combination of halitosis and BO was too much and Jane was ready to run away. 'Look,' he said, 'It begins peacefully enough just like any other sunny day in Athens.'

Jane stood up with her handbag on her shoulder, 'Please, why don't you sit down?' She offered him her chair and took her jacket off the back of it, folding it over her arm.

'Hundreds of students. Comrades, brothers and sisters.' He continued to scroll, 'Here is their leader, preaching to his disciples. One wonders what exactly was being said that was so revolutionary and inciteful that they had to shut him down?'

Jane was about to leave quietly when she caught the image he was pointing at out of the corner of her eye and came back, 'Wait, show me that one again!' She pulled up another chair and put her jacket and handbag down on the floor next to her. OK he was younger with long hair but the muscular frame, the deep-set dark eyes and the Minoan jaw were all identical. Jane got goose-bumps and shivered in trepidation. 'What's this man's name?' She touched the screen and felt his gaze, the man who had beaten her up and nearly killed Daddy. 'Do you know anything about him?' Jane reached into her handbag for a notebook and pen and making proper eye contact for the first time waited for Che's answer.

'Known simply as Demetri, he's Greek, from the Central Highlands originally. At this time, I mean during the 1970s he was notorious and very active, a leading light we could say in the Leftist Nationalist movement,' he paused.

'So what happened?' Jane transferred her glance from her pen where she was poised to keep writing and the would-be Marxist guerrilla leader whose name she didn't even know yet.

'He went underground, and then all we have are rumours. We thought that either he was turned or killed. But…'

'Still alive then, you think?' Jane knew he was alive.

'Oh yes, definitely. I mean from time to time he surfaces or should I say something that seems like him or is redolent of his methods appears in the newspaper and you think, "Yes," he is alive.'

'Does he still live in the mountains, I mean is he still an activist?'

'Ah, what do I know?' He raised both palms skywards and shook his head, and would have laughed out loud if they weren't still sitting in a library. For the first time she noticed his nicotine-stained fingertips. 'But, listening to the people over the years, he doesn't live in the mountains any more. He stays on one of the islands when he isn't doing business in Europe.'

'What kind of business? You seem quite well informed.' Jane hoped that flattery might help tease the answers out of him.

'Oh, well, no not really. I just read a lot. They used to say Karpathos, but I'm talking twenty, maybe twenty-five years ago so who knows. But definitely, from your research this is the most interesting figure, and that is the photograph you should ask for a copy of.'

'Thank you…?'

'Petros,' they shook hands and he was gone before she could say her name.

Jane was a bit flabbergasted that her research had proved so fruitful and she left the ancient harbour feeling full of emotion for the small part she was playing in such a big historical picture. Back in Piraeus she sat down at one of the corner cafés to smoke and drink a beer. She also ordered one of the large pizza slices which looked so good in the serving hatch window. Piraeus continued apace unabated, people both tourists and Greek were coming and going plus a new influx of European refugees, taxis, mopeds, motorbikes and buses all driving fast and stopping just as quickly as the plethora of traffic lights turned red. And the port beyond the high fence busy at a much slower pace with much bigger vessels, the larger ships dwarfing whole sections of the city. One family caught her eye, Mum and Dad plus two kids who seemed to be in their own happy bubble, their love for each other protecting them from the sometimes cruel world surrounding them.

Much to her surprise the Ariadne had new guests. Jane was pleased for her hosts who had shown her nothing but kindness since she arrived. Jane's siesta was punctuated by the sounds of laughter and children running up and down the corridors, but she didn't mind. When she woke up and came out after showering to go and buy beer, it turned out to be the family she'd seen earlier on in the day, as is so often the way with these things. They were sitting at the low white table in the foyer playing cards and Papa was standing up studying the sailing map.

'Hi, do you want to join us?' It was the mother and her accent sounded Dutch.

'Yes, come come come!' It was the girl who must have been four or five Jane thought pulling her tee-shirt imploringly and jumping up and down.

'At least come and have a drink with us?' It was the father still studying the map and his cards. He discarded two cards and picked two up. 'Have you eaten already?'

'Oh, thank you, I'm not really very good at cards but maybe you can show me?' Jane said to the little girl, 'Let me go and put these in my fridge. I'll be right back.'

At that point Ariadne appeared from nowhere and said 'give me those' in Greek, indicating that she would keep them cold and then she said in English, 'Sit, sit.'

'OK I get it, you guys are teaming up on me so that I don't spend any more time alone in my room, is that it?' Jane laughed and opened a beer.

'How did you guess?' the mother said.

'Cheers,' the father raised his beer.

'Bravo,' Ariadne pushed through her little flap-door and started to put cutlery and plates on the table.

'You will join us for supper? Please…' the father let Jane sit down. 'I'm Yan, this is my wife Marieke, our daughter Heidi and son Raiph. From Holland as you can probably tell. And you are?'

'Jane, from England. Nice to meet you all, I saw you earlier in Piraeus.'

'Ah yes, we are stranded really. Our boat broke down.'

'Again,' Heidi laughed.

'You're on holiday?' Jane asked.

'We live on the boat, year round. We are intellectual gypsies!'

'Hippies,' said Mum.

'Pirates,' said Heidi.

And Raiph giggled, still being shy. Ariadne bought bread and a large Greek salad plus a little saucer of tzatziki. She placed a large bottle of mineral water and two large bottles of beer on the table and wiped her hands on her petticoat.

'Kali orexi, eat! I bring more when it is ready,' she smiled and went back in the kitchen. The kids dived in and mum helped them to dish up.

I've still never seen Mr Ariadne Jane thought abstractly, 'Excuse me, let me go outside and smoke.'

'Smoking's bad for you,' Heidi said with a mouth full of bread, clearly concerned.

'Don't mind her! Sorry we Dutch have few filters, even the children,' Mum berated Heidi.

'Come back whenever you're ready,' the father helped himself and then passed the plate to Mum.

As Jane sat outside in the night, smoking and drinking her beer she knew it was time to move on. John wasn't going to pass through Piraeus by accident, she could see that now and it made more sense to go straight to Karpathos. With or without John she was going to confront Demetri and end this thing. The smell of the main course reached her nostrils and she went back inside for an evening of Dutch and Greek hospitality, whether she liked it or not.

Raiph was tired and full and getting sleepy. Heidi was plaguing Ariadne by running in and out of the kitchen in order to be chased out again squealing.

'Let me try and take them to bed,' Marieke said. 'Night darling, say goodnight to Papa! Goodnight Jane, see you in the morning.' She picked up Raiph and Heidi followed still giggling and squealing and dancing round and round.

Ariadne cleared the plates. 'It was delicious, thank you!' said Yan.

'Yes, thank you Ariadne,' complimented Jane.

'Let's take coffee outside and you can tell me your story.' Yan went to order at the desk and came back with two more beers.

CHAPTER SEVENTEEN

The next day Jane woke up with a sore head and a dry mouth. She couldn't remember the end of the evening very clearly but was relieved to wake up alone. Did they? Had they? She wasn't sure of anything except the recollection of needing to get drunk and being grateful for the opportunity to offload. How much had she told him? Did they go anywhere else after the hotel?

She showered and then went a bit sheepishly to breakfast and greeted Ariadne. Was it Jane's imagination or was her smile a little more conspiratorial than usual? Oh, God, she thought shamefully and wondered what might have happened. But she was a good girl and soon shook it off. She sat at her favourite table outside and watched the gigantic port waking up, getting her thoughts in order.

'Hi Jane, are you hungover like Papa?' Heidi ran up to her and gave her a big hug, she came from the street so must have been somewhere already, maybe the boat Jane thought.

'Morning Heidi, where have you been so early?' Jane asked.

'We went to see our boat and Papa had to jump in the sea to wake up! Bye.' Heidi waved and skipped off going inside the hotel just as Yan came round the corner carrying two blue plastic bags of groceries.

'Morning Jane,' Yan smiled, 'And don't worry about last night, you were great, I mean funny, I mean it was great. I'll shut up!' He laughed and shook his head. Then changing the subject, 'They've fixed our engine, one of the securing bolts had sheared off, but it's sorted now. So we're leaving this morning.'

'Oh wow, that was quick,' said Jane still wondering what the hell she could have done the night before.

'You erm still want to come?' Yan sat down and seemed to sense her fragile state.

'What?' Jane spluttered, spilling coffee on her chin.

'You told me about Karpathos and we're heading to Rhodes so you can come along and be an extra crew member. Besides it's good for Heidi and Raiph to have a friend for a few days. Up to you; Marieke says it's fine.' He carried on inside.

Jane was sad to say goodbye to Ariadne who had been so sweet and there was an awkward moment when the older lady asked about her passport. Jane said quickly, "Keep it in the safe for me if it comes but I'll try and call them to rearrange delivery." They hugged and both knew she was lying.

'And the money for the other nights?' Asked Ariadne.

'Keep it, I may come back! Efcharisto poli.'

'Kalo taxidi!'

'Yassas, yassou, bye!'

157

The five of them ran and skipped along Piraeus' busy pavements like one big happy family. The boat was a cross between a fishing boat and an anti-U-boat launch from WWII, the antithesis of what Jane would have wanted to cruise the Mediterranean Sea in. She was even moored side on, instead of stern on to the dock like the more glamorous vessels, to accentuate her ugly lines. *Pandora* was predominantly grey, probably an undercoat of some sort Jane figured and part of her cockpit's canopy was a patchwork of handwoven reeds. The bits that weren't grey primer were fluorescent Netherlands orange; in short she was as eccentric as her owners.

The family lined up like sailors of old and piped her aboard with Marieke playing the recorder, 'Welcome aboard, Captain Jane,' they chorused and even Raiph was enthusiastically clapping.

'Come,' said Yan, 'let me show you to your quarters.'

'Don't worry Papa, I can do that!' replied Heidi enthusiastically pulling Jane's hand, 'Come on!'

Below decks was noticeably neater and homelier than what Jane had seen up top so far and she assumed it was Marieke's influence. 'Oh, it's so lovely!' she said out loud.

'Look,' said Heidi jumping up and down, 'this is where me and my brother sleep.' She swung into a hammock suspended in a little steel-framed room painted wall-to-ceiling with safari animals and jungle foliage themes.

'And this is where we all go pee-pee and poo-poo,' she showed Jane the heads and carried on the tour past the master-cabin, orange and Dutch but cosy and liveable Jane thought and forward to her berth. Just big enough to sleep in and contemplate life or death but not unpleasant, this time painted with scenes of sunsets and waves – dolphins, whales, seals and walruses. It must have been an alternative bed for whichever child couldn't sleep or had maybe misbehaved.

'You can leave your bag,' said Heidi and she took Jane back towards her family. 'Oh,' she said, 'this is the kitchen. On a ship we call it a galley I think in English?' She scrunched up her face in puzzlement and then they went up the steep steps into the sun again.

'Karpathos here we come!' said Yan raising his hands in the air, 'Darling?'

Marieke jumped to mock attention and summoned Jane to join her untying the ropes fore and aft which still attached them to the dock.

'I can do it, I can do it, please Daddy!' Heidi was crying and screaming without tears.

'No, baby, you stay with me. Somebody has to steer the ship remember?' said Yan, holding on to his daughter tightly. Raiph was securely ensconced and strapped into his sea-cot.

CHAPTER EIGHTEEN

From Gibraltar the fastest and most direct route to Greece during the summer months is the southern route passing between Malta and the southern tip of Sicily. If stops in Malta or possibly Sicily were kept short we were still looking at another eight to ten days at sea. I estimated the eight hundred nautical miles to Malta would take a week and then maybe forty-eight hours sailing the additional two hundred and eighty-one nautical miles at approximately six knots from Sicily to Greece. The biggest unknown was the weather as this stretch of Ionian Sea can be unpredictable with sizeable storms and waves plus any mechanical issues would mean having to stay in port longer for repairs. I hadn't decided where to enter Greece yet and wasn't even sure which island Demetri called home. I just knew I had to find him and make it right for Peggy.

Arthur meanwhile had gone from taking it all in his stride to not enjoying it at all and I was worried that he might be ill. Fresh out of port I was still enjoying bread and salad and treated myself to a Mediterranean feast at the end of our first day's sailing. The dog enjoyed his Spanish dog food as the sun set on a calm sea, the calm after the storm, and I tucked into my Greek salad, olives and calamari drinking cold retsina and listening to the second test on long wave. The sat. link allowed a now daily update from Mike who had told me to expect further documents via fax. I waited for the machine to start clicking as England closed the first day in a good position for once, having lost only three wickets. Sailing solo without the adrenalin of being pursued was exhausting, constantly on watch even when I allowed myself some sleep with the autotiller in charge I found I was going a bit doolally and hallucinating not about Peggy, but about Jane. Was it a fatherly interest I had in her or something more primal, more carnal? I hadn't fallen in love since meeting Peggy in the 1970s nearly forty years ago so the emotions I was now experiencing were quite discombobulating.

The fax machine started to chatter and I poured myself another glass of retsina, put Arthur in his basket and made sure he was securely tied up and took the tiller, making sure that I was also hooked in. The current and the wind were both with us and I let out the main sail and a genoa. I wouldn't be able to try and read anything until our speed had reduced a little bit, as we were pushing eight knots. These were long sailing legs and I wouldn't get much rest even with the autotiller turned on, which is a bit like trying to run as fast as you can in a straight line with your eyes closed and trusting to instinct that you're not going to hit anything. After years of sailing I was getting better at it but being alert to the possibility of the autotiller failing and dozy rather than confident and comatose was a much better lifesaving policy which had paid dividends in the past. The biggest danger after the weather and big seas is huge container ships and oil tankers who may never even know that they've capsized you in the worst case scenario, as they plough on relentlessly unable to stop or alter course within a two kilometre window. I settled down to enjoy the seven and a half knots we were now pulling and admire the day's waning rays of light. We still had birds for company, sea gulls, shags, even owls, but they would be gone back to shore soon and then it was just us and the occasional dolphin pods – always a welcome sight at sea.

161

PART THREE

CHAPTER NINETEEN

Thanks to Mike I now had a bit more to go on, and the fact that he was sending classified information to a retired friend raised more questions than it answered. Putting aside any doubts I absorbed what he had sent while we burned some diesel and motored along through an unusually calm stretch of Ionian Sea. Arthur had come up top to join me and I was relieved to see him feeling a bit better.

By sending me this I got the sense that Mike had thrown in all his cards. I might not be getting the whole picture of his personal involvement but ours was a game of nuances a bit like cricket, and even if the hints were subtle they weren't imaginary and might affect the outcome of the game, or even the series. I made sure the gennaker was ready in case a light following wind picked up and I could raise it, gave Arthur his dog food (still Spanish) and sat down with an unspillable mug of coffee and a tuna mayonnaise sandwich.

The new file wasn't from the Department, although the source had been blacked out I could tell it was American, FBI or CIA. Mike would know that I would deduce that so again the sense of finality. It started with the familiar biog. and the introduction of a codename Pegasus. Born in the central highlands, educated by monks, clever enough to leave the village and go to university in Athens to study law. Left-wing nationalist beliefs, possibly communist. Radicalised, or at least mobilised after the death of his brother who was a petty-thief and armed criminal back home. Came to the attention of the secret services in 1973 during the Athens Polytechnic uprising. This was new information and I looked at the attached black and white photograph. It took me back to a time early in my career and a world, and a Greece that seemed lost in the depths of time, yet it also reminded me of the man whose fist had crashed into my cheek and whose actions had directly or indirectly caused the death of my wife. There were economic and business conferences all over Europe and reports of a successful legal career. Pegasus dropped off the radar in 1986 amidst rumours of a move to Karpathos, marriage and a conversion to traditional Greek Orthodxy. Recent activity: possible Pegasus involvement in the assassination of the ex-US Ambassador in Athens.

Didn't resurface I thought to myself, until he telephoned me a week ago. Poor Dan, I remembered the old American from the good old days. I finished my sandwich, gave the dog some water and couldn't decide between crisps, fruit or digestive biscuits for my pudding. I went with crisps thinking I could always have fruit and biscuits later at tea time. With a change in the wind and slight cloud cover I cut the engine and let out the gennaker.

CHAPTER TWENTY

Demetri was barefoot and bare-chested on Pigadia's sandy beach loading his clinker-built kaiki with everything he needed to shut down his island. The boat was his pride and joy, repaired many times by his own hands, all the strakes and topside planks had been cut and shaped and replaced by him. He had saved it from fiery extermination and if he hadn't actually built it from scratch his blood sweat and tears were as much a part of its construction as the wood, pitch, paint and metal which held it together were and he loved it as he would a son or daughter. The supplies he loaded seemed innocuous enough but there were no prying eyes here, he had earned the right to do as he pleased on Karpathos by quietly building and decorating so many churches and shrines. There were staves and boards for signage as well as planks, wire and paint that would help him to build a temporary landing stage. He also packed scuba diving tanks plus mask, flippers, and wet-suit, just in case. His harpoon gun, food and fresh water, also camera, notebook and digging tools that he might need to excavate and record the burial tomb if the appropriate archaeological authorities couldn't come before the inevitable dénouement.

Once fully-loaded Demetri pushed the boat out into chest-high water which was hard with the added weight and she gave way only reluctantly with an audible sigh. As the kaiki slid along the bottom towards deeper water he climbed on board to sit with his back to the open ocean and take up both long wooden oars, made by him, in his strong hands. What armaments he still had, guns ammunition grenades were already cached on the island and he put his back against the strength of the ocean knowing that this might be the last trip he ever made. Demetri said a silent prayer to the patron saint of the island, Mary the holy Mother of Jesus and another prayer to Katerina and his dearly departed brother to whom he dedicated all of his many actions, good or bad. And lastly he asked Saint Nicolas the patron saint of all sailors to bless him on this his final voyage.

Once into the bay proper he raised his sail and Demetri's keen eyes watched the port's comings and goings with interest. The cruise ships would offload their passengers and for a few hours Karpathos would again be inundated with souvenir hunters and restaurant customers and lovers looking for secret beaches and secluded rocks. The marina was also busy with only one or two vacant yacht berths, he flinched momentarily as he watched a beautiful brunette in a bright bikini top and khaki shorts waving excitedly at the arrival of a boat with a dog on deck. For a second he thought it might have been them but a water taxi sped past and obscured the view.

At To Nisí Demetri landed the kaiki on a small stony beach in the cove where he had already built a lean-to structure, into which he now decanted the boat's contents. From here he would sail back round to the promontory and start construction of the fake anchorage and put up the signs. Any daytrippers, fishermen, tourists or property investors would now know that there had been an outbreak of an unknown virus on the island and that the local municipality had declared it a no-go zone signed by the mayor of Karpathos, anyone with symptoms should contact their local G.P. and stay quarantined at home. The hand rails and boat rings would be daubed with the virus and he himself would then stay away from that part of the island, going up into the hills to build a more secure shelter where he could hideout, excavate the ancient burial site and, if necessary, defend his island.

He spent the first night with a simple fire at the mouth of the cave. He ate bread and beans and fried some fish he had caught earlier. There was some red wine which he drank from a horn cup he had made in a previous life. Let them come, he thought, as the sky burned like fire, I am ready. He thought about John who had done as he asked and prepared the virus but now he wanted revenge for the death of his wife. Demetri could understand his motivation. Mike would come for the reward money and might also fight to keep his land now that it was worth millions of dollars. But we'll see who gets the island and has the last laugh, Demetri lay down and slept.

In ten years of coming here to build and then visit his chapel, to swim and fish here and guard the secret cave Demetri had never once seen boats docking. With the exception of the Andrianakis Consortium's visit. Once in a while people moored and swam over to dive off the rocks but that was about it. Until now. Demetri woke up to see two boats both trying to tie up to his new jetty. One was the investors who looked as though they'd come armed with lawyers this time. Why couldn't they have found me at home Demetri wondered? And the second was a dinghy from a strange looking ship which was half-grey and half-orange, probably Dutch tourists he thought. Demetri had seen a family in the port a couple of days ago and figured it was them. Couldn't these people read Greek? He didn't know what to do. The brave warrior decided to hide and pretend he wasn't in hoping they would go away. But if they docked and came up the ladder they'd get the virus and be killed...he had to think of something.

Demetri climbed down from his camp to the hidden bay where he'd overnighted the kaiki and grabbed some materials from the lean-to. His first thought was to take a couple of grenades and scare the living daylights out of them but that seemed a little ruthless. Instead he took a facemask and goggles from his tool box and picked up one of the skull and crossbones signposts he hadn't put up yet and ran round towards the landing stage bursting out of the trees and shouting, 'Danger, Danger, not safe, deadly virus!' He coughed for effect and stood at the end of the jetty shooing both boats away. There was a brief moment of defiant hesitation and then common sense prevailed.

Demetri had done enough for now and he watched them turn around (albeit in some confusion) with relief, in the belief he'd saved their lives.

CHAPTER TWENTY-ONE

'You're a hard woman to find,' an unshaven mixed race man in sunglasses and a leather jacket sat down opposite her.

'What the hell are you doing here?' Jane demanded.

'I know you don't believe me but we really are the good guys. EUROPOL.' He showed her his ID again and this time it seemed to make more sense. Jane was speechless and she lit a cigarette. Giovanni ordered a beer for himself and one more for her. 'If it helps I think John is also one of the good guys.'

'Who's going to help you catch the bad guy,' Jane said defensively.

'That's where it gets complicated. You should go home and save your life.' Giovanni finished his beer and examined the receipt in the little Ouzo glass, he left enough euros to cover their drinks plus a tip, and put them under the glass.

'What do you mean? Are you going to arrest me?'

'Unfortunately I can't tell you and I can't arrest you without a warrant. All I can do is advise you.' He took off his sunglasses and looked her in the eye as if to say "be careful" or "do the right thing," and then he was gone again.

Jane saw *Oystercatcher*'s mast and John's silhouette long before they even docked, as a speck on the horizon threading itself through the gap in between two mighty cruise ships like silk through the eye of a needle or floss between a giant's teeth. She sipped her frappé sketo and lit the first cigarette of the day. Her plan had worked, the gamble had paid off as she knew it would, female intuition and all that, and now she glowed all over in anticipation.

She ran from the bar where she'd been waiting down to the marina where she expected John to dock. She'd said her fond farewells to the Dutch family two days ago when they arrived in Pigadia. Her hosts' natural bluntness had made goodbye easier thwarting Jane's instinctive British reaction to be upset. Yan and Marieke had both thanked her for helping them and then it was three pecks on the cheek and 'Bye!' Heidi had of course been a bit sad, but hugged Jane and said, 'I hope he loves you! I hope you get the baddie!' Raiph gurgled and said a lot in his own language but nobody could quite yet understand what he meant. *Pandora*'s non-geometric shape and bright orange colours weren't visible in the marina this morning so perhaps they'd already sailed on to Rhodes or Mykonos.

Jane found *Oystercatcher* just as she was backing into her berth and started to wave frantically, 'John, John! Hello Arthur, hi baby!' Arthur started to bark and wag his tail in excitement and John too was beaming from ear to ear. What a welcome, and what a beautiful bay he thought. The sun didn't yet reflect back off the clear blue sea and the whitewashed hills and buildings of the port, it merely saturated them with colour and made everything seem richer and deeper. It was already hot and there was no real breeze to speak of and Jane felt that even the sounds were

169

accentuated, the twin motors gurgling in reverse, Arthur's barking but at the same time she couldn't hear anything at all, focussed as she was on John; the man who had saved her life. Finally the docking was complete and she jumped on board.

'John, Oh God, I missed you so much I don't know how to say it! I'm not usually like this.' Jane was shaking and fumbled for a cigarette which she lit and took a drag of. She grinned a big broad smile which he hadn't seen before. 'Silly of me,' she said, 'I should have said something. I'm in disguise, you probably don't even recognise me with this hair.'

John took it all in, took all of her in. He didn't know what to say and desperately didn't want to say the wrong thing. 'It's OK,' he managed, 'I feel the same,' and involuntarily he too revealed to her a deep-down smile. He held both of her hands and their eyes met in silence for a moment. She came inside his embrace and kissed him full on the lips and they hugged tightly for the first time. It was magical; him smelling her perfume, deodorant, cigarettes, feeling the softness of her skin and her breasts her heart beating, her feeling the boniness and the strength in his upper body, the faintest hint of aftershave from three weeks ago, and the pheromones given off by a man who lives outside, the wool of his jumper, the sea.

Just as I was starting to think about finding the harbour master he found us, a short swarthy man who was all hair and beard beneath a very weather-worn baseball cap. I expected him to have no legs as he approached in his little wooden rowing boat but stand up he did with legs like short tree trunks protruding from yellow shorts about the same age as the baseball hat. He greeted us warmly in Greek but made it clear that he was a polyglot and we could conduct our business in any language. I chose English more out of habit than anything else not wishing to reveal to a complete stranger that I too could speak many languages.

'I already know your business,' he announced unexpectedly but without any animosity.

'That's the small island you're after,' he pointed to his left to the far north of the island, and we had to physically turn round to see the shape of To Nisí in the distance.

'But there's bad news, I'm afraid,' he continued before we could voice our amazement. 'They say there's some disease over there, a deadly virus. My advice would certainly be to stay away. Have a good day and forgive me for interrupting,' he blushed briefly.

The harbour master handed back my papers and jumped down from the dock into his little skiff to row away again like a sort of prescient goblin. Scare tactics? Or maybe he was simply showing off, perhaps the bush telegraph worked well here but no, a more probable explanation was that we weren't the first foreigners to ask about the island and he was simply flexing his muscles in front of Jane. We should probably spend a day or so in Pigadia getting a feel for the place and maybe find out what the locals thought. I already had a vague idea where the mysterious virus might have come from.

Jane wished the Dutch family were still here so that she could introduce them to John. She told him all about her adventures as they walked along the harbour-front and he told her about their voyage, although it had been pretty uneventful. Arthur ran along but was still a bit wobbly from so long in the boat. It was still early but the cafés were open for coffee and breakfast or something a little stronger for some of the fishermen. Deliveries of fresh fish were being taken off the boats coming in and heading off to the restaurants and minimarkets.

'Do you want to stop and eat something?' We were walking arm in arm and I didn't really want to stop promenading but breakfast might not be a bad idea.

'Sure, that one looks nice!' Jane pointed to a corner café with long awnings and cushioned wicker armchairs. We sat down and they immediately brought Arthur a bowl of water and he was happy as soon as he realised what it was and that it was for him; and menus for us. The waitress hovered for our drinks order. Jane ordered a frappé sketo and I ordered white coffee.

'Shall we get breakfast as well?' I asked hungrily.

'You can,' Jane lit a cigarette, 'I'm far too excited to eat.' She looked me in the eye and laughed, 'I know, I'm a wreck.' And she giggled to herself again.

When the coffee came I ordered scrambled eggs on toast with orange juice. 'This is a beautiful island, isn't it? Have you been here before?' I asked sipping my coffee and stroking the dog's ears.

We weren't the only customers, maybe half a dozen tables had people and the waitress, a young austere

172

Greek girl was busy running up and down between them. Behind us two old men sat with their backs to the café wall were playing chess but I couldn't hear any of their conversation it was too muffled. In front of us a black British family were busy playing at the end of what looked like a big breakfast. Judging by the luggage they were headed home or at least leaving the island, and waiting for a ferry.

'No, it's my first time. Yes it looks lovely. You can stroke me too you know?' Jane teased. 'There's a famous mountain town isn't there? The Dutch family were telling me, Mount Olympos?'

'Yes, it's stunning, I went there years ago. Bit of a climb, though, even in a car I mean. The road's really steep. Maybe we should go up there and have a look?'

'Well, if I was a fugitive I wouldn't be hiding in the port, would you?' Jane took a sip of my juice said, 'Oh, that's good!' and went back to her cigarette.

The eggs were delicious and I gave the crusts to a grateful Arthur. I asked the waitress about buses to Olympos and she looked at her watch as if to say it's a bit late to set off now. She said a taxi would be much better but it takes about two hours to get there, the bus three hours. I paid the bill and we thanked her.

'John, let's hire mopeds, look I found a place on my phone.' Jane said showing me the picture. 'Arthur can stay on the boat can't he?' she asked.

'Or we could all stay on the boat and sail to Diafani, which is stunning and right below Olympos. We can spend the night there, it's even on the way to To Nisí.'

173

'I'm in your hands,' she grinned, 'if you know what I mean?'

We bought supplies at one of the mini-markets; including some big juicy peaches which looked and smelled delicious. Back on board Jane showed off her boat prowess from her time on *Pandora* and we were cast off and gliding out of port in no time.

'It's probably a bit early for lunch,' she said sidling up to me at the helm in her bikini, 'what are we going to do for the next hour John?'

I put my hand gently on her waist and felt a tingle of electricity surge through my body as she kissed me. 'Perhaps we'd better moor up somewhere,' I said stupidly. But Jane wasn't in the mood for such practicalities as she helped me to undo her bikini.

Diafani was indeed stunning, the one-time port of ancient Olympos it was now an eco-tourism destination but modest with its fame and not at all overcrowded. The crystal clear blue waters were too much for Jane who dived in gracefully at the earliest opportunity.

We stopped to have lunch just beyond the horseshoe-shaped natural harbour in a beautiful gulley between high naked rocks. Here a sequence of inlets and coves are connected by channels deep enough to sail through and we really felt as if we'd arrived in paradise. Arthur was tempted to dive in but I think the height of the jump from the boat to the sea was too daunting. Being able to see straight down to the bottom probably didn't help, and there were plenty of bottoms that day.

Back at Diafani we thought about hiking up to Olympos with the dog but it was now so hot that a moped was still the order of the day and with me driving and Jane's arms wrapped tightly round me we sped off uphill. It was only a five kilometre climb and the bike had no problem carrying us but the gradient nearly defeated it a few times as the engine changed tone from deafening to barely audible and then nearly dead a few times. We did manage to stop half-way up at what looked like a newly-built chapel to St. Thikon. We enjoyed the shade of the almond and olive trees and found the church door open, inside smelled of fresh paint, candle wax and dried flowers. We lit candles and said our own private prayers and marvelled at the brightness of the gold leaf and red paint on all the painted panels. We drank water marvelling at the view below us before getting back on the bike.

Olympos was far more impressive than I remembered or maybe it was just the company I was with but we were both suitably gobsmacked. We parked up outside a café in the main square and its proprietor welcomed us and we soon had no alternative but to sit down. Jane lit a cigarette and smiled broadly, flushed from the hot climb but still looking adorable. I dreaded to think what I looked like but tried not to worry about it. The café was a tables-outside extension of the local bakery staffed mainly by middle aged Greek women of an indeterminate age and seemingly infinite knowledge. Either that or they made tired-of-life look like wisdom, I couldn't tell which.

As the one who'd encouraged us to sit down in the shade approached and said 'Good afternoon, welcome. Something to drink?' Jane took the lead, 'Hi, we just came from a beautiful church which looked brand new. Would you have any idea who built it and when? We'd love to compliment the architect and artist.' I was instantly charmed and it seemed so was our host as she went off to discuss our question in a loud voice with her colleagues.

'His name is Demetri, and you can find him here,' she lifted an arm to indicate Olympos, 'or down in Diafani.'

And there he was: Pegasus revealed. I was speechless. Jane ordered two beers, a village salad, kalamari and chips. Our waitress returned with the cold drinks and some bread. I had no idea how I was going to eat again but eat we did and it was absolutely delicious. Our quest more-or-less complete we rode down to the harbour in a relaxed fashion and found Arthur alive and well. With no need to eavesdrop in expat bars for information we enjoyed a delayed siesta and wandered out as a threesome much later on when it was already dark.

Diafani was more pedestrian than Pigadia, the island's capital, but by ten p.m. there was a quiet buzz about the place and one or two of the bars were getting lively with boat crews enjoying cocktails outside and the cooler temperatures. The young Greek men, boys really, were out in force showing off their moped and motorbike skills to the girls who sat unimpressed waiting to be bought a drink or taken somewhere in a car, bored of Diafani. I thought I could stay here forever with Jane by my side. Retirement in Greece, it had a certain ring to it, but what would Jane do for a living? We'd reached the far end of the beach now and left the crowds behind us. The darkness here felt like a cool cotton sheet and the music from the bars just a memory.

176

'Look,' Jane said pointing and shook me out of my daydream. We stopped walking and my gaze followed her arm to a traditional kaiki which had been pulled up onto the beach for off-loading, attached to a long painter. Lit by moonlight the curly black hair of its owner shone silver and gave him the countenance of a much older man. He'd grown a goatee also shot through with flecks of white, but it was definitely him we both felt it and Jane stood rigid. He was too preoccupied with his task of bringing boxes ashore to take any notice of us.

I reached for my trusted Browning but wasn't wearing it. Before I knew what was happening I ran across the beach and threw myself at Pegasus in the shallow surf. The impact took us both underwater and even though I'd got a good choke hold round his neck stronger arms than mine wrestled free and held me under. In no time at all I felt myself drowning and that's all I remember.

CHAPTER TWENTY-TWO

It came to me in the night with a rather naked Jane draped across my shoulder. A sudden flashback to Cambridge in 1986: I was playing cricket with work as part of a Scientists XI, brought in no doubt for my somewhat deadly left-arm slow bowling. Panayota was also up from London as it happened, and her cousin was part of the visiting team named The Bengal Tigers although they were a hotchpotch of visiting academics and not all Indian by any means. So we had met, I could see him now twenty-five years younger with long black hair under a headband, wearing a gold ear ring I seem to remember. I also remember he wasn't the only player wearing sweatbands and fluorescent socks. The stubble was already there and the same square jaw but the grizzled features of today were merely Ottoman Empire back then. It was a two-day game and Demetri came on at the end of Day One as a nightwatchman, and I got him out first ball the next day, caught and bowled. Apparently I'd made an enemy for life.

I shook my head, how was it possible that two of the world's biggest intelligence agencies had failed to notice that one of their most wanted men was related to one of their employees? I supposed it was just life and had to laugh, I also felt that Panayota would not necessarily have known anything about her cousin's illegal activities. I mean if he'd kept it hidden from us why share it with his relatives? Jane came back from her morning skinny dip and stood smiling and dripping on the transom. I was losing my appetite for guns and killing and gaining an appetite for Jane. She wrapped herself in a sarong and starting to prepare breakfast.

'What happened last night? How am I still alive?'

'EUROPOL,' Jane said biting into a piece of bread and apricot jam. 'My guardian angel, a black man called Giovanni saved your life. Pegasus went free but we were too busy doing CPR and getting you back here.'

'Wow.'

'A very handsome black man, actually.' Jane threw in casually, teasing me. For a moment I wished I was dead as the pain of jealousy tore through me.

Jane must have seen the look on my face and came over to console me, 'You're still my hero, John, don't worry.' And then she went back to the galley, 'How do you like your eggs?'

CHAPTER TWENTY-THREE

Mike told Dorothy that he had to attend a blasted training course in some god-awful hotel and she took it on the chin as she always did already planning which girlfriends to invite where before she'd put the phone down. He was actually on a plane to Cyprus from where he would be transferred by Westland Sea King helicopter to HMS Richmond who had been pulled out of manoeuvres in the Gulf of Antalya to steam at full speed to the Mediterranean. Mike's boss had made it very clear that this was make or break for him and if anything at all went wrong he was a) on his own and b) could kiss goodbye whatever retirement honours he might have expected from the PM.

CHAPTER TWENTY-FOUR

We left the crystal clear waters of the bay for a deeper ultramarine sea as we approached To Nisí less than one nautical mile away. From a distance it looked like so many other wooded islands in Greece, out-of-bounds and probably owned by a millionaire somewhere. Through the binoculars there was no sign of any building apart from a shrine on top of the highest point and ruins of possibly a monastery or castle slightly lower down. I could see a landing jetty with the KEEP OUT signs that the harbour master had warned us about but no other signs of life on first inspection.

'He has to be there,' I said to Jane as I put the binoculars down, 'I can't see his boat but I just know he's there waiting. If not for us for whoever else has been asking questions.'

Jane came and cuddled me, she was wearing a short-sleeved shirt over her bikini, 'So what do you think he's hiding?' She asked, 'Or is it simply time for one last stand?'

'That's what we're going to find out. Whatever it was that brought him out of hiding after twenty-five years he thinks is important enough to kill and be killed over.'

'What do you think John?' She was looking at me in a funny way.

'I think that the island holds a secret and somehow it has to do with what I and Mike, the British

181

and the Americans were all doing here in the 1970s. Beyond that I don't know.'

'Have you got time to take me below before we go and find out?' Her shirt was already off and mine was being surreptitiously unbuttoned as we fell down the companionway towards the cabin.

Avoiding the infected harbour which we knew was a ruse I put *Oystercatcher* into a sheltered cove that hid the boat and gave us access to the shore. A lean-to shelter on the rocks showed me that Demetri also docked here but today there was no sign of a boat. I decided to leave Arthur on board, partly because it was going to be too hot for him and the terrain was pretty foreboding. With a bit of luck he might also act as a guard dog for the yacht, 'Cheerio, old boy. Look after her!'

Jane and I swam and waded ashore and climbed onto the rocky island. I carried the rucksack and we headed uphill on a narrow path which was punishing from the start. Ascending steeply through the rocks and thorny bushes we were soon out of breath and longing for a change of terrain, it eventually came after about thirty minutes and we reached a natural clearing of sorts. From here we could see the sea on the side we'd approached and above us the ruins of some sort of castle or monastery. We began to see why the island was never inhabited, or at least not for very long.

'Keep going up?' I asked Jane, trying to find any sign of a camp or a structure that Demetri might have put up.

182

'Looks like it,' she said. 'At least from the top we might get a better view of the whole island. Try and work out where he is?'

'Sounds good to me!' We set off again after sipping some water and the path this time was thankfully less steep with fewer rocks and thorns to scratch our legs. We entered a mini pine forest and took in its warm scent, enjoying the shade. On the other side of it we came out onto a ridge which allowed us to see both sides of the island for the first time and to our surprise we found the grey hulk of a Greek warship lying at anchor off the opposite coast.

Another ship hove into view approaching from the south as we had done, maybe two miles away and I checked it through the binoculars and was surprised to see that this one was British. We were sandwiched between two navies with a maniacal tyrant. Suddenly there was a whoosh of air and something big, the size of a dining table or a piano sailed through the air high above us and thudded into the treeline above. Nothing happened for a few seconds and then Bang! the whole ground beneath us shook and a deafening roar reverberated between the mountain walls above us and rocks and trees split and tumbled in our direction. Fwump, and another one whistled in.

This was naval shelling, completely unexpected and fearsome in its power coming as it did from ships we could barely see. Were they Greek or British shells? Jane and I couldn't tell but so far the range was off, they seemed to be pounding a ridge in between the beach and the highest monastery and so far the only casualties were trees. We would have to move quickly or be killed and I

183

opted for back uphill given that the sea was now part of a naval battleground. As we climbed, Jane's tight shorts stayed two steps ahead of me. I thought to myself that this was now an international incident and wondered cynically if that was what Mike had wanted all along, a private war? I was just a disposable pawn, to be discarded once my usefulness had expired. Jane by association would also be deniable and I knew now that there would be no more help from the Department. That realisation was almost a relief; like Demetri, I was a lone wolf who worked better unfettered.

The rocky terrain was difficult to cover quickly moving as it did every time a shell hit but we soon found ourselves back on the ridge and above the worst of the bombardment. Tucked underneath one of the overhangs was a cave, which we'd both seen at the same time.

'John, look!' said Jane, 'Let's go and check it out.'

I didn't know how much shelter the cave was going to offer if it took a direct hit but it was better than being out in the open. As soon as we entered we found signs of Demetri who was obviously preparing the cave for something. Inside a second chamber I heard Jane gasping out loud, 'Wow, John. I think you'd better come and look at this.' I followed her voice deeper into the rock and sure enough we found ourselves in an elaborately decorated burial chamber.

'So that's what this is all about,' I said, after a brief and breathless exploration of Demetri's find we were sitting at the cave mouth to take stock.

'It's so beautiful and exciting, Oh my God!' Jane kept saying and she lit a cigarette staring into the middle distance and smiling. It was her turn to daydream.

'Come on,' I said. 'Let's keep going.'

The abandoned monastery was the only other shelter for miles and although it might be an obvious target for indiscriminate artillery the walls were thick and it at least offered a good view of the island.

'Phew, we made it!' Jane put her arms round my neck and we both felt our hearts beating faster as we clung on to one another and got our breath back. She kissed me and smiled and I thanked the monastery's patron saints for delivering us safely.

'Have we still got water?' Jane danced around my backpack and pulled out one of the chilled bottles we'd packed for the hike. 'Thanks' she said then she sat on a rock outside and lit a cigarette. The shelling seemed to have stopped or else they were adjusting their range. I sat down next to her and admired the view. The main headland stretched out in front of us, Demetri's cave just below, the Greeks on the right and the British to our left. *Oystercatcher* was hidden in a cove on the British side and would be safe I thought unless they sent a launch to try and land.

'What's the plan?' Jane asked not unreasonably.

'Gut feeling?' I replied, 'let them have Pegasus. We should concentrate on getting out of here alive. This island will be swarming with marines from both sides soon if I'm not mistaken.'

'But this is the guy who hacked off my dad's hand and killed your wife. Are we just going to let him go, having come all this way?'

'I don't think he was personally responsible for either Peggy or James although indirectly of course I can certainly blame him.

'Maybe there's been enough death already,' I said putting my arm around her. 'There's too much at stake now, I can't risk anything happening to you.' I took back my arm and waited looking out at the light bouncing off the chalky rocks and the turquoise sea beyond.

Jane stood up and walked forward three paces still with her back to me. I couldn't bear the suspense. Then she turned round and said, 'Oh John, I think that's the most romantic thing anyone's ever said to me.' She bent down to my level and brought her hands together behind my neck, her tanned breasts either side of my face. The shelling started up again and shook the ground beneath us.

Our climb hadn't been in vain because we'd found the tomb. What we hadn't found was Demetri but To Nisí was fast becoming a dangerous place to be. We drank more water, ate some chocolate and decided to get back down to *Oystercatcher* as quickly as possible.

Back at the boat we weighed anchor and I started the engines. Jane came up through the hatch with her arms in the air, 'Darling,' she said. I could tell straight away from her eyes that something was wrong.

186

'It's not darling, I'm afraid,' a familiar voice said with a pistol pressed into the small of Jane's back, 'I hope you don't mind but it seemed like the only way to get off the island.'

Demetri had sneaked on board as a stowaway; I saw red and span the wheel hard to port, which on a starboard tack brought the boom swinging round with a jolt. I managed to duck and pulled Jane down with me but it caught Demetri square on the forehead. Even Arthur got involved snarling and biting at his shins but Pegasus was out cold, alive but unconscious. I put him in a lifejacket and dumped the body overboard firing a flare to alert both navies and it was done.

'Well I guess we got our revenge,' I said. 'The authorities can deal with him now,' but something wasn't right and I knew it. I was meant to deliver Demetri to the British or the Greeks all along but why? Who was calling the shots? It had to be Mike. I didn't really understand why yet but I knew it was him and I'd been a pawn in his game, and Peggy had paid with her life. I thought about the American report he faxed and the death of our old friend the ex-Ambassador. Whose payroll was Mike on? Mike had used me to get to Demetri and it was personal, not official that much I knew. While I thought Mike was doing me a favour meanwhile… meanwhile I now realised that Mike must be a double agent. It would have to wait until another time, I was exhausted.

'Yes, we did baby, thank you,' said Jane and she went to change into her bikini, declaring when she re-emerged, 'I think I'll read my book on the foredeck if anybody needs me!'

We both laughed, and I said, 'Aye aye captain! Dressed like that I shall probably be needing you quite soon...'

Arthur looked at me with his head at a jaunty angle and I opened him another tin of Spanish dog food.

THE OXFORD BOTSWANA MURDERS

AN AMANDA GODSPEED NOVEL

Nick Green

When the murdered body of a Merton College undergraduate turns up in the centre of Oxford, Detective Inspector Amanda Godspeed from Kidlington must investigate her first murder case. All the clues point to Botswana, Africa and Amanda is drawn into a world she had never even dreamed of. The case, although deadly awakens in her something that will never go away: Is it a feeling of wanderlust or something deeper? As they race against the clock to avert further catastrophe Amanda is forced to question all that she once took for granted.

TEZCATLIPOCA'S DREAM

A MEXICAN NOVELLA

Nick Green

In search of his biological father, Henry finds himself in Guanajuato, Mexico, where he falls in love with two women, Jenny and Dina. Increasingly jealous of his new best friend Buck's friendship with Dina, Henry stands on the edge of an ancient abyss. The netherworld is calling him

Tezcatlipoca's Dream is a journey into the Lord of the Smoking Mirror's parallel realm, Nick Green brilliantly reinventing the Mexican novella in this immaculately drawn study of life, love, death, and resurrection.